THE FIRST HUNT OF PHOENIX GREY

A GREY SISTERS SAGA NOVELLA

CRISTINE COURCY

SMASHED HOUSE PUBLISHING LLC

For you.
Thank you for taking a chance on me.

CONTENTS

THE RECLUSE

She left before the sun came up.

I watched her go. I couldn't help it. And then I couldn't go back to sleep. So, grumbling to myself about the ungodly hour, I stuck my wand into my topknot and stumbled to the kitchen for breakfast.

Icarus, my mother's black cat familiar, watched me from the counter as I fired up the coffee machine and rummaged through the cabinets for a mug and an apple cider donut. The cottage was quiet...

It was never quiet.

I scowled moodily into my mug before I stuck it underneath the coffee machine.

Everyone had left. But wasn't that what people did? You'd think I'd be used to it by now.

"She didn't have a choice, Phoenix." Icarus's ears twitched as he watched me. "She had to leave."

I glanced sideways at the cat. I plucked up my mug,

sloshing coffee down the sides, and took a big bite of donut. "Which one?"

Icarus flicked his tail testily, his fur bristling. He had no patience for me.

The feeling was mutual.

I smiled sweetly at him over the top of my mug. "You'd rather Phin was here instead of me, huh?" Everyone preferred Seraphina. And I didn't blame them. With her golden hair and bright smile to match, she was as pleasant as sunshine...and I was—what'd she always call me? A Labrador? I flashed a lopsided smirk and tossed my dark hair out of my eyes. I'd take it.

Icarus regarded me coolly. Then he jumped off the counter, disappearing through the kitchen doorway into the living room.

"Well, too bad!" I called after him through a mouthful of donut. "You're stuck with me."

The silence of the cottage answered me.

It wasn't just Phin who was gone...our little sister, Fawn, was staying with our grandmother until our mother came back from some secret task handed down to her from the High Council.

The High Council was the secret organization in charge of policing the magical community and keeping us hidden from nonmagical people. We didn't know much about them, other than the fact that they took over sometime in the 1800s, drafting laws for the witch community that, if broken, resulted in medieval-level punishments.

As Icarus had needlessly reminded me, Mama hadn't

wanted to go, but if the High Council tells you to do something—you do it.

Or else.

I guess.

With a heavy sigh, I took my mug and donut out the back door, onto the porch. The one good thing about waking up so early—at least I could appreciate the sunrise over Nile.

Our family cottage was nestled in the heart of the little island town, on the outskirts of a forest, the back porch overlooking endless fields and a small glimpse of the water. There was nothing like the sunrise over the tree line, spilling into the fields, or the sunset burning just beyond the lake.

I tried to enjoy the calm of the new dawn, but all I could think about between bites of donut that stuck in my throat and gulps of coffee that scalded my stomach was that Seraphina, my sister—my *twin* sister—had decided she was done with homeschool. She wanted to go to school with regular kids, like our friends Cole and Rachel. Without me.

She said it was because of magic. Being a home-schooled witch learning the craft is kind of hard when you don't have any magic to work with...and she didn't. For whatever reason, unknown to anyone, Seraphina had been born without magic.

So going off to school with boring, regular kids and pretending that magic was just, well, pretend...that'd make sense. It'd be totally understandable...*if* that was her real reason for wanting to leave home.

But it wasn't.

I knew better.

I knew the *real* reason she wanted to get away. Even if she was too ashamed to say it out loud. Whatever. It sure wasn't because she wanted to be "ordinary" and "normal." No witch in her right mind would want that.

I finished my coffee and donut just as the cold October sun stretched out over the top of the trees, setting the burnt leaves ablaze.

Time to get to work.

I pushed off the porch and headed back inside. I went to our room and dug out my Book of Shadows from underneath a pile of dirty clothes. I dropped it on the bed and flipped through it to the last page, trying to remember what I was working on last week.

I frowned at Friday's entry...the Forging Ceremony. Right. My heart sank uncomfortably into the pit of my stomach. Seraphina had done the impossible: she'd failed to forge a wand. Never before in history had a witch failed to forge a wand. But she'd done it—or rather, *hadn't* done it, and I had. Which just gave her more of a reason to leave.

So she said.

I slipped my wand out of my topknot and ran my fingers over it. I hadn't really looked at it, or even held it since the Forge. I couldn't bring myself to after what Seraphina had gone through...it'd felt cruel. But now, in the quiet of the cottage, I marveled at its beauty: the black-red of the smooth magical iron, with the gold and orange markings swirling around it like thin ribbons.

I bit my lip as a smile tickled the corner of my mouth.

Now was as good a time as any. I scooped up my Book of Shadows and headed outside to try out my wand.

It wasn't necessary, a wand. Witches could cast spells and work magic with a finger just as well as with an instrument—if not better. It was one thing to channel magical force through the body, another entirely to channel it through a magical object on top of that. So, although wands made the magic stronger, they also made it more difficult to perform.

In the olden days, wands were our weapons, but now, thanks to the High Council, the warring between witches was over, and the Forging of Wands by sixteen-year-old witches beneath a Hunter Moon was merely ceremonial... a rite of passage, rather than an essential step for survival. Now almost all witches kept their wands as a symbol of status, rather than as a tool they actually learned to utilize. Because it was hard. Wandsmanship was an almost impossible skill to master, so not many did. My grandmother, High Priestess of the House of Grey, was always quick to say wands became crutches. Wands made witches lazy.

But by Merlin, they were *fun*.

I spent the rest of the afternoon perfecting my incaendium spell. It was a personal favorite of mine. Incaendium was a tricky spell that, when done correctly, shot a sliver of fire from the tip of your finger. Let's just say, I wasn't given the title of Phoenix the Red because of my hair dye. And that spell...with a wand? *Awesome*.

Over and over, I cast the spell until finally I could point my wand and shoot fire into the pit with near perfect precision. By the end, I was hot and sticky, my forehead slick with sweat, cold in the fall chill.

I shook my hair from my eyes. Last one. "*Incaendium!*"

Fire blasted from the wand, roaring as it hit the pit, and burned out on impact. I grinned. It was a spell I could always do easily, with just the point of a finger, but never had I ever cast an incaendium spell as strong as that. The wand boosted my magic from a flame to a blaze. It was incredible. It was—

"Wicked!"

I flinched at the voice. I turned away from the fire pit, breathless from the effort, and squinted up toward the porch.

Fawn hopped down the steps to meet me.

"That was totally awesome!" She grinned up at me, her blonde curls blowing in the cool breeze. "Do it again, Nix!"

I grinned. Hex yes, it was awesome. I ruffled her hair and pushed her head off to the side. "Nope." I stuck my wand back in my topknot. "Time for your potions."

The laughter died on her face. Her golden-brown eyes darkened, and she kicked at the cold grass. "Do we have to?"

"Yup." I led the way up the porch steps and held open the door for her, as she trudged her little lanky self into the house.

"But Phin isn't even home yet," Fawn grumbled. She gathered her things from the hutch and dropped them onto the kitchen table. She plopped down into a chair, giving me a moody stare.

I shrugged and grabbed another donut. The box was almost empty. I'd have to go to the store tomorrow. Jinx it. I glanced at the clock as I took a big bite. "She should be."

Fawn cocked an eyebrow. "She *won't* be, will she?"

I waved her question away with my donut. "How's Grammy?"

Fawn blew her honey curls out of her face. "Fine."

I leaned against the counter. "That's all I get? *'Fine'*?" I made a face as I munched my donut.

"*Fine.*" Fawn rolled her eyes, a hint of a smirk on her rosebud lips. "Grammy's great...but she keeps shoving books in my face. Keeps going on about how I'm a 'rare talent.'" Fawn dropped her chin into her hand.

"Well, that's cool—"

"It's annoying," Fawn snapped. She fiddled with her mini cauldron. Copper sparks of her magic sizzled in her hair.

I struggled to hide a smile. Rare talent? Fawn was a *powerful* talent. At eight. How strong would she be at sixteen? And with a wand of her own? I smirked. Very cool.

"What?" Fawn's honey-hued eyes narrowed. She glared at me from across the tiny kitchen.

"Nothing." I grinned. "Let's get to work."

Before I could drop into the seat beside her, the phone rang loudly. We both flinched.

"Is it Mama?" Fawn sat up straight in her seat.

I frowned and made my way to the phone. The caller ID flashed on the side.

"Who is it?"

I inclined my head as the phone continued to ring, shuddering in its base. "Nobody I know…"

"Answer it!" Fawn pipped.

I glanced back at her, an eyebrow cocked. "No."

Fawn rolled her eyes. "Why not?"

I tossed the last bite of donut into my mouth and spoke with my mouth full. "Because it isn't for me. And it sure as hex isn't for *you*. So that means it's for Mama, and she isn't home."

Fawn started to protest, waving her hands at the phone. The ringing stopped. Her arms fell, as did her face. "Now we'll never know who it was!"

I smiled sweetly. "Potion time. Fire up the cauldron."

Fawn groaned.

I laughed.

"Where is Mama anyway?" Fawn lit the bottom of the small cauldron with a prod of her finger. She glanced at me sideways as she set up the scales. "What is she doing?"

I snorted. "Cut your octopus brains."

Fawn hacked up the brains impatiently. "So, you don't know, either."

I scowled at her sass. "What I *do* know is—"

Icarus pounced onto the table, startling the both of us. "Someone's coming."

My heart leapt into my throat. I pushed up from the chair. Our two best friends Cole and Rachel were at school with Phin. Aside from them, we didn't have visitors. We had pranksters...or worse. "Ding Dong Ditch the Wicked Old Witch Down Old Grey Lane" was a favorite of the island kids. They never made it far up Grey Lane, our long driveway that cut through the woods. Only one had ever made it to the door.

And although everyone knew witches didn't exist (ha!) and magic wasn't real (heh...), our family seemed to bother people...a lot. Which was why we kept to ourselves...even more than the average witch. Because unlike most witches who had overall anonymity, in addition to the protection of the High Council, our family was one of the twenty-two Hallowed Houses. The Hallowed Houses were coven families, established witch bloodlines that had endured through the centuries until they'd become legend in the simple minds of the mundane.

The Grey name was infamous in Nile. And islanders never forgot that their great-grandmother's grandmother saw Constance Grey walk on water, or that their grandfather's grandfather was struck drunk by a love potion from Elizabeth Grey. And they never forgot to tell their children the ghost story of *The Wicked Old Witch Down Old Grey Lane*. And *no one* could ever forget that they used to burn Greys on Bird Island, a tiny rock off the west shore of Nile. We were hated, not visited. So, suffice it to say, someone showing up in our driveway—not good news.

Fawn made to follow me.

"Stay." I waved my hand, and she was forced back into her seat, my magic glittering around her like orange pixie dust.

Fawn stuck her tongue out at me as I ran to the living

room. I pulled back the curtain. An old truck emerged from the woods, rumbling violently over the potholes, and came to a stop in the wide gravel drive in front of Grey Cottage.

Two guys got out and headed for our front porch.

"Fawn!" I shouted. "Pack up your potions. Back to Blackwell. Now."

2

IF YOU'RE JAMES DEAN, I'M AUDREY HEPBURN

I leaned against the front door, eyes closed, weighing my options. I had about thirty seconds before they made it to the door.

Icarus sat at my feet. I peeked at him.

"He's a friend of your mother's from the old days..." Icarus said dryly. "And it appears as though he passed through her warding enchantments. You can let him in—if you want to...but I wouldn't."

I cocked an eyebrow, interest piqued.

Icarus padded away toward the bedrooms, his tail flicking with irritation.

My ears prickled at the sound of heavy boots on the porch steps. I smirked to myself. This could be fun.

I threw open the door.

"Bad idea," I snapped sharply. I leaned lazily against the open doorframe, arms folded across my chest.

They hesitated halfway up the steps, clearly caught off guard.

Ha. Excellent.

I took the second it took them to recover to look them over. They looked like different versions of the same song —obviously related. The younger one, not more than eighteen if I had to guess, was taller than the older one. With fancier hair, short on the sides and swished back like James Dean. And grumpier, too. His sharp, angular face squinted up at me with a hint of annoyance that matched my own.

The older guy had the decency to look embarrassed. "Uhh—"

I regarded them both with bored indifference. "You got ten seconds to tell me what you're doing here before I start hexing."

The younger guy scoffed and shot a look at his buddy, who held up his hands, his eyes on me.

"My name's Traven DeVarney..." He pointed to the younger guy. "This is my kid brother, Logan. We're looking for an old friend of mine—Charlotte Grey?"

I shrugged. "She's not here. You can go now." I pushed off the doorframe and started back inside, but he didn't move.

"Do you know where I can find her? It's really important..." Traven's forehead wrinkled, as he flashed me a hopeful smile.

I frowned, considering. They had passed through Mama's warding...which meant they weren't a threat.

"Listen, uhh—Ms. Grey? Er, Blackwell?" Traven took a tentative step forward.

My frown deepened.

"I'm assuming you're a—a cousin, yes?...and I know you want to keep Charlotte safe—but there's something she needs to know about the Dark One."

I cocked an eyebrow. My frown slipped for a second. Okay. He had my attention now. I pursed my lips, trying to maintain my cool exterior. "The Dark One..." I inclined my head, as though I knew what he was talking about.

I totally didn't.

Traven nodded, his face serious. "And her demons—"

I nodded slowly, as though my heart wasn't pounding and my thoughts weren't racing. Demons? Did he just say *demons*? Like metaphorical? "Right...well, that sounds like something Charlotte definitely needs to hear—come on in."

I held the door open for them and watched them with a grim, haughty air that would've made my Great-Aunt Cordelia proud.

Traven gave me a polite smile as he slipped inside and headed straight for the kitchen. He'd been here before. Logan didn't bother to look at me, his annoyance chiseled in his sharp features. I shut the door and followed them into the kitchen.

I went to the cabinets and grabbed a mug. "Coffee?"

"Absolutely, thank you." Traven took a seat at the table. Eyes on Logan, Traven jutted his head toward the chair beside him. Logan sighed and dropped into the seat with a surly expression.

I flicked the machine and pushed the mug underneath. My ears prickled as they whispered between themselves. I turned around quickly, leaning against the counter, and eyed Traven expectantly.

He gave me an uneasy smile. "I really think I should tell Charlotte when she gets back…"

I crossed my arms again. "Okay, well—I can tell her you stopped by…"

Traven's eyes crinkled with amusement. A smirk slid onto the side of his face. "Point made."

I smiled. I plucked up his mug and slid it in front of him. Then I plopped into the chair across from them and waited.

Traven took a sip, his eyes closed in appreciation. He set down his mug and cleared his throat. "I don't know how much you know about the war with the Dark One and her demon army—but there has been an increase in activity of dark witches down in Louisiana, and—"

Logan snorted as he leaned back in his chair, folding his arms across his chest. "Dark witches? A bit redundant, don't you think? I mean, they all go dark eventually…"

"Dude—" Traven shot him an impatient scowl.

Logan smirked and gave a lazy shrug. Then he dug into his pocket and pulled out his cell phone, which buzzed and blinked in his hand. "Excuse me. I should double check the mandrake tranqs." Logan shoved his chair out from the table and left the room.

I blinked stupidly, still trying to comprehend what Traven was attempting to explain.

"Heh. He's kidding…chucklehead…" Traven scowled at his brother's retreating back. Then he returned his focus to me. His expression softened. "A few days ago, on a hunt, we were able to get it out of one of the younglings...they believe the Dark One has risen again. And what's left of her demon army are amassing to try—"

Suddenly, Icarus jumped onto the table and padded across it to sit in front of Traven, inches from his face.

"Icarus!" I scolded. "Off!"

He ignored me and spoke to Traven, who leaned back in his chair, clearly taken aback. "Charlotte Grey won't appreciate you discussing this with her daughter, Mr. DeVarney."

Traven peeked around the cat and stared at me, wide-eyed. "*Daughter*?" He choked and coughed. He pressed his fist into his chest. "I thought—wait, *what*?"

My cheeks burned. Busted. I grinned guiltily and shrugged.

Icarus stood from where he sat and padded along the tabletop to face me, his tail lashing from side to side. "And you, Phoenix Grey, should be ashamed of yourself."

With that, Icarus leaped down from the table and disappeared through the doorway. I rolled my eyes and pushed back in my chair. I went to the cupboard for a donut. My face fell. Last one. I tossed the empty box into the trash. Taking a bite, I dropped back into my seat.

Traven ran a hand through his thick, sandy hair. "You're Charlotte's *daughter*..."

Traven gulped his coffee.

"One of three, actually." I smiled, my cheeks packed with donut.

He choked again.

I took another bite.

"You were saying?" I mumbled around the donut.

Traven put down his mug with a firm shake of his head. He held out his hand. "Nuh uh. Nope. I'll wait to talk to—to your *mother* about this, thanks."

I grinned cheekily. "You'll be waiting awhile. She's Unreachable." I popped the last bit of donut into my mouth and smiled sweetly. "So, you might as well continue...I'm most interested to hear about demons—I didn't realize anything like that even existed. And you said you hunt—*what* do you hunt, exactly?"

Logan walked in the room just in time to catch my question. He stood just behind his brother and watched me with a cool stare. "Witches."

My eyes narrowed.

Traven glared up at his brother from his seat. "*Dark* witches... *Wicked* witches..." He turned back to me with an apologetic smile. "And demons, and—"

"Other monsters," Logan added with an ironic smirk.

My fingers curled at my sides. I wanted to hex his face.

"Other *evil* things," Traven corrected loudly as he stood abruptly from his seat and put a hand on Logan's chest. "Why don't you go check on the truck, little brother. Now."

Logan rolled his eyes. "Fine."

I watched him leave, fighting the urge to hex him in the back.

Traven cleared his throat as he sank back into his chair. "Sorry about the kid. He's had a few bad experiences with witches in the past—"

"You don't say?" I muttered dryly.

Traven gave me a weary smile. "Listen, uh—Phoenix? I first met your mom when I was on a demon hunt with my dad as a kid—like twenty years ago? She's an old friend—we keep in touch now and again, and I just wanted to warn her—there might be serious trouble brewing—"

"She's Unreachable," I interrupted flatly. "The High Council called her away last night."

Traven sat up straight in his seat, his eyes wide and alert. "The High Council? Are you sure—"

I stared at him. Of course I was sure.

Traven nodded, acknowledging the stupidity of his question, and he stood slowly from his seat. "Then it must be true...okay, well—thanks for the coffee, Phoenix..." He flashed me a quick smile that crinkled his eyes and gave me a small wave before he abruptly left the kitchen.

Scowling, I jumped up after him.

"Wait a minute—where are you going?" I demanded, following him out the front door and onto the porch.

"Charlotte's Unreachable, so I'll have to go warn her myself," Traven called back over his shoulder without stopping.

I just barely kept up with him as he made it to his truck. Logan leaned against the truck bed, squinting at us as we approached.

"Wait, how do you even know where to find her?" I snapped impatiently.

Logan's eyes flickered between the both of us. "What's going—"

Traven jutted his head toward the truck. "Let's go, kid."

Logan scoffed, shaking his head. He wrenched open the truck door and hopped obediently into the passenger seat. The truck door creaked and slammed shut.

Traven gave me another quick wave. "It was nice to meet you, Phoenix. Oh, er—Logan will be at the By the Lake Motel if you need anything. He's not as much of a jerk as he seems, so really, reach out for help if you need it..."

"Wait, what—" I stalked around the side of the truck after him, but Traven didn't stop.

He jumped into the driver's seat, swung the door shut, revved the engine to life, and left me fuming in the driveway in a cloud of dusty gravel.

TERRIBLE THINGS

I spent the rest of the evening poring through every book in the cottage. There wasn't a single mention of demons or monsters in any of them. Apparently, Mama had carefully curated our collection, omitting anything that might even *suggest* the existence of supernatural beings, evil or otherwise.

My face hurt from frowning so deeply as I combed through our catalog...but I couldn't help it. How could she keep something like this from us? A demon army? And what in the hex was a Dark One? Was there a Vader-type villain lurking in Louisiana?

I glanced at the clock above the fireplace. It was late. My eyes slid back to the book in my lap. *Phin* was late.

Icarus jumped onto the couch and curled up at my side. Instinctively, my hand went to his soft fur. I stroked him gently as I turned the page. Icarus's steady purr vibrated against my leg, calming me instantly.

"If your mother wanted you to know...she would've told you," Icarus mumbled through his purrs.

I glared down at him from the corner of my eye. I slapped at another page. Before I could snap a retort, Icarus's ears twitched beneath my hands. Both of us looked up toward the front door. Car lights. Seraphina was home.

I scowled pointedly down at the book and slapped at Icarus's head. A few moments later, the door opened and the glow of the headlights disappeared.

I didn't look up.

She hesitated in the doorway, as though she wasn't sure she was welcome.

Perceptive, my sister.

She shut the door gently. "Hey..."

"Hey." I turned the page and continued slapping at Icarus's head.

"Did Mama call?" Seraphina prompted softly.

I kept my eyes fused to the page so hard the runes began to blur. "Nope."

"Okay...I have a lot of homework—so, I guess, I'll see you later?"

I didn't answer. By the time I snuck a peek, she'd disappeared down the hallway to our room. I didn't join her until I'd finished skimming the stack of books on the floor at my feet.

Scowling, I tossed the last one onto the pile with the rest of them.

Icarus sat up on the couch, his claws kneading the cushion as he purred.

I looked down at him sideways. "Don't be too happy... I'm raiding Blackwell Manor in the morning."

Icarus flinched and looked up at me with narrowed eyes. "You will do no such thing."

I grinned with a tilt of my head. "I will. And you can't do anything about it because Mama's Unreachable."

Icarus's tail flicked. "You know *I* can still reach her—"

"But you won't." I patted his head, hard. He glared up at me. I smiled my sweetest smile. "If Mama's Unreachable, and there really are evil demons and dark witches and Dark Lords involved—that means it's dangerous. And *that* means you aren't going to bother her unless it's serious, life-or-death...and me nosing through an old library is hardly life-or-death."

Grinning, I gave him a final crude pat and hopped from the couch. "See you in the morning."

My smile vanished as soon as I reached our bedroom door at the end of the hall. I'd been so obsessed with finding information about demons, I'd buried the hurt I still felt about Phin. All of it flooded back as soon as I stepped into our room.

I gritted my teeth and went straight to my dresser for my pajamas and left the room to change. Even my most comfy pjs couldn't brighten my mood. And that was saying something. I was a firm believer in the healing power of comfy clothes.

I stomped back into the bedroom and tossed my wand on my nightstand. I snatched up my book and jumped into my bed and buried my face in the pages of *Frankenstein.*

But I couldn't focus.

I was seething.

For some reason, all I could think about was where she'd been all evening. While I was digging through a mountain of books, what had she been doing with Cole and Rachel? Suddenly, my stomach hurt. It wasn't that I was jealous—I'd rather get a hex in the face than go to some stupid school—but she hadn't been at school for hours...what had they been doing?

I glanced sideways at Phin. She scribbled something in a notebook and stuck her nose in another. She'd dumped all her school stuff all over her bed. And there she sat, right in the middle of the mess of textbooks, notebooks, writing utensils, and even a set of pom-poms. And she called *me* sloppy? I snorted despite myself.

"What?" she snapped.

"Nice pom-poms." I snickered.

She snatched the pom-poms and tossed them under her bed.

So, she was a cheerleader. "Figures," I mumbled under my breath.

"Do you have something to say?"

I didn't bother to look up from my book. "I just can't believe you actually signed up to be a cheerleader." I shook my head as I slapped at a page, and said dryly, "Congratulations, you're officially a walking stereotype."

"How does being a cheerleader make me a stereotype?" she demanded.

I slapped another page and said with sarcastic sweetness, "Now you just have to start dating the captain of the football team and you'll be a cliché." I looked over at her, my caramel eyes cold. "Fawn was really hurt when you didn't come home."

And I was, too.

I slammed my book shut and snapped my fingers. My lamp went out with a little pop. Then I flopped over, turning my back on her, and glared at the wall for hours until I finally fell asleep.

The next morning, I slept in...a bit.

Until lunch.

Squinting through my sleepiness, I stumbled through the cottage. The sun streamed warm and bright into the kitchen through the window in the back door. I fumbled around the cabinets, looking for something sweet. Nothing. I grumbled along with my stomach and abandoned my search. I stalked back to my room to change.

Settling on a pair of baggy black pants with too many pockets and an oversized Hawthorn Heights T-shirt, I smiled slightly at my reflection. My black hair was a mess, the dyed orange tips sticking out in places. I tilted my head and fingered the bright-orange ends. After Halloween, maybe I'd switch it up...dye it all a black-red or something...choppy streaks like Gale Weathers in *Scream 2*. I shrugged at myself, gathered my hair into a messy bun, and stabbed my wand through the center. Comfy clothes were key to a good day, but fun hair didn't hurt, either.

I grabbed my backpack. The sight of it instantly

improved my mood. Rachel and I had decorated each other's backpacks with tons of enamel pins and keychains. It was the little things, you know? It never took much to brighten my day. I smiled. Time to go.

I went to the kitchen for a passage candle. Icarus trotted after me and rubbed against my ankle with a small mew.

I rummaged in the drawer for an orange taper. "Don't think you can sweet-talk me into staying here to rub your belly." I held the thick candle in both hands and nudged him with my toe.

Icarus hissed. He leaped up onto the counter and watched me with critical eyes.

I gave him a coy wink before I rubbed my fingers over the candle wick. It sparked and sizzled with glittery orange magic right before it popped into flame. The candle literally lighting my way, I opened the back door of the kitchen and stepped outside.

Instead of the back porch, my feet landed softly on the small wooden dock jutting out from the rocky shore of Grey Isle. And instead of the backyard and the woods in the distance, a big, sloping, grassy hill rolled up to the sky. And there at the top was old Blackwell Manor.

A cold gust of wind rushed all around me, extinguishing the candle and showering me with icy lake spray. I shivered against the cold, cursing myself for not grabbing a hoodie. But it's not like I could go back for one. The cottage was no longer behind me; only the gray churning waters of Lake Champlain were at my back.

Blackwell Manor, the ancestral home of the House of Grey, was built in the 1800s after our family was driven off by the islanders, back when ordinary people still believed in the extraordinary. We were forced to settle on one of the smaller islands that surrounded Nile. Grey Isle was then founded.

Grey Isle itself wasn't much, just a grassy hill, with a bit of woods at the base, that stretched up high and then plunged violently in a steep cliff, as though a piece of the island had been hacked away into the lake. But Blackwell Manor was our refuge, a sacred place for the whole extended family, and although most of them had moved mainland, it was an actual home to my grandmother, Nancy Grey, High Priestess of the House of Grey.

The manor was an architectural marvel—strange, yet beautiful to behold. It was a jumbled confusion of Tudor windows with their timber frames, medieval castle turrets and stone, and Victorian steeples and balconies. But even more strange was how the manor sat: so precariously close to the cliff that it seemed dangerously impossible. So much so, that boats would often pull up beside the tiny island just to stare up the cliffside at the manor. The sight was so bizarre it'd make you blink your eyes several times, in an effort to verify your vision. Nile legend had it that the manor was held up by magic, for what else could explain why it didn't crumble into the lake? Little did they know, it probably was.

Though the world had stopped believing in magic and witches, in large part due to the High Council cloaking our society in secret and policing our people with a medieval fist, the family never went back to Nile...except for Mama.

For some reason, Mama had gone back. And she was the only witch to set foot on Nile's rocky shore in a hundred years. She never fully explained why. But that was Mama. Everything was a need-to-know basis, and we just had to accept it.

And Seraphina did.

I didn't.

Which was why I stood on the dock, shivering my butt off in frigid October. I hitched my backpack farther on my shoulders, wincing underneath the weight of it, and marched off the dock. Eyes on Blackwell Manor, I trudged up the soft dirt path that curved up the hill.

I didn't accept being kept in the dark. And I was going to get to the bottom of this, no matter what Mama said. Or didn't.

4

IN TOO DEEP

"Phoenix Grey—aren't you a sight for ancient eyes." Grammy had her arms around me in a tight hug as soon as I'd walked through the doors. I squeezed her back even tighter. She pulled away from me and held me at arm's length. She was a tall, delicate woman, but with such power behind her striking silver eyes. I shifted uneasily beneath her critical gaze. She pursed her lips and eyed me suspiciously. "My girl...what on earth are you up to now?"

My cheeks burned. I flashed her a guilty grin. "What? Can't a girl visit her grammy on a Tuesday afternoon anymore?"

Grammy crossed her arms and cocked an eyebrow. "Not this girl..."

I chuckled, as I dropped my passage candle on the side table. I glanced around the entrance hall. "Where's Fawn?"

Grammy's arms fell to her sides. Her face warmed.

"Oh, you know Fawn. She's running loose in the woods... she'll be back in time for dinner, I'm sure."

I nodded. "All right, well...I'll be in the library."

Grammy raised her eyebrows, taken aback. "The *library*—?" Her eyes narrowed. "Why...?"

I shrugged lazily. "To study! Why else?" I flashed another cheesy grin and gave her a quick wave. Then I disappeared down the hall before she could call me back to remind me that I'd never studied before in my life.

Although I didn't study (ever), I did read. A lot. Although what else would I do—it's not like we had a TV. Either way, I appreciated a good book, and the Blackwell library had a billion of them.

The library of Blackwell Manor was always impressive, no matter how many times I stepped inside it. Books, hundreds and hundreds, lining shelves from floor to ceiling, covering the walls completely. A large fire burned brightly in the fireplace against the far wall. And the cushy chairs and couches positioned prettily around the room made it all come together in an odd mix of cozy and spooky. I tossed my bag into a chair, went to the card catalog, and got to work.

It didn't take long for me to find something unusual —*nothing* unusual. I found nothing. It was the same as Grey Cottage...as if all the books had been carefully curated and combed of any out-of-the-ordinary topics. I was hungry and increasingly cranky by the end of it.

"Can I help you find something, Phoenix the Red?"

I glanced toward the double doors.

Uncle Richard had peeked his head inside, resting his hand on the doorway. A thoughtful smile, half hidden in his wild beard, crinkled his kind eyes. I tossed the book I'd been skimming onto the pile without bothering to close it.

I sighed, giving him a rueful smile. "No, thanks, Uncle Richard...and you don't need to title me—" With the Wand Forging came a ceremonial title based on our magical talents...Phoenix the Red...a coven Elder addressing me as such...made me uncomfortable.

Uncle Richard chuckled as he walked over to me. He surveyed the mountain of books on the coffee table between us. "Looks like you've got quite a question on your mind..."

I scoffed. "You could say that."

I hunched farther down into the cushions of the couch and kicked my feet up onto the coffee table. I gave him a sour smile and hugged a plush couch pillow to my chest as I studied him.

Uncle Richard Blackwell, Grammy's brother, was one of the Elders of the House of Grey, but he dressed like he was an ancestor. With his three-piece suit, waistcoat, and overcoat, Uncle Richard wouldn't look out of place in a 1920s fashion magazine. He was balding on top, with the sides of his head cropped short in tight black-gray curls. What hair he lacked on his head, he made up for on his face. His neatly trimmed beard was thick and bushy and often hid his smile, giving him an extra air of mischief when his eyes crinkled. Like it did now, as he peered down at me.

He gave a quick glance at his pocket watch, before tucking it neatly back into place. "You know…" Uncle Richard tossed his coattails behind him and slipped his hands in his pockets. Rocking back and forth on the balls of his feet, he looked around the library, nodding thoughtfully as his eyes moved over the shelves. "Back when I was a boy, if ever I had a question that I couldn't answer…I would find a good book and search for answers in front of the fireplace."

I sat up a bit straighter in the poofy cushions of the couch.

Uncle Richard nodded again, his mouth downturned in a thoughtful frown. "Yes, indeed." He clapped his hands, rubbing them together as he smiled down at me. "Well, I am late for a meeting with your great-aunt and grandmother. I shall see you, Phoenix, yes?"

With that, he gave me a small bow. Then there was a whoosh and a flutter, and Uncle Richard vanished in a whisp of gray smoke.

A smile slid onto my face.

I knew I loved him.

I didn't waste any time. I chucked the pillow aside and hopped from the couch. Light on my feet, I hurried to the double doors. The hallway was empty. Quiet as I could manage, I heaved the heavy oak doors shut. Then I leaned against them as I scanned the library. A good book. What did Uncle Richard consider a good book? I frowned thoughtfully, enjoying the riddle. *The* Good Book was the

Bible...that could be it...the Bible provided answers... Or maybe it needed to be a book *I* thought was good? Like an eye of the beholder kind of thing?

I went for the Bible first. There was an extensive selection of Bibles, different editions from several different centuries. Some with leather bindings peeling in places and gilded pages, and some with hand-painted lettering...what did they call it? Illuminations? I scrunched up my face. Finally, I snatched the Bible that looked the oldest, figuring if Blackwell Manor had a secret, it'd be from the founding, which meant the book would've had to be around back then...maybe? I brought the book over to the fireplace.

The warmth from the fire made me smile. Gingerly, I cracked the Bible open. On the first page was a little inscription that read, *"For Constance on her Wedding, February 2nd, 1822."*

I began to pace the length of the fireplace. Back and forth. Over and over. Nothing happened. I chewed on the inside of my cheek as I delicately flipped a few pages and continued to pace. I turned back to the note. There was a small subscript at the bottom. It was in Latin. Great. I blew my bangs out of my eyes. I could read it—maybe. But I had no idea what it meant. Phin was the language scholar, not me. I barely knew all my runes.

I cleared my throat. I licked my lips and scrunched up my face. Then I stumbled over the words, my tongue thick in my mouth. *"Scientia, aere perennius, scio me nihil scire."*

I walked the length of the fire while I spoke. I turned on my heel and walked back...

And stumbled.

I inhaled sharply, hugging the open Bible to my chest, my eyes wide on the floor.

Or rather, what *had been* the floor.

A staircase had formed beneath my feet, leading down in a coil into the depths of Blackwell Manor. My heart hammered. I glanced quickly toward the library doors. I looked back down at the spiraling staircase, my sneakers planted firmly on the first step. A smirk snuck across my face. I didn't have to think twice.

Gently, I placed the Bible on the mantel and hurried back to the couch for my backpack. Then I crept down the stairs, slowly and cautiously. They were steep and there wasn't a railing. The steps themselves were slightly slick, as though they were wet from some kind of condensation. I kept one hand on the stone wall as I moved down into the bowels of Blackwell Manor.

It was cold. So cold it felt damp.

I blinked rapidly, attempting to adjust my eyes to the darkness. But as I made my descent, a low glow emanated from below, spilling onto the last few steps.

I stepped out of the stairwell. My breath caught in my chest. My eyes widened as I struggled to take everything in at once. It didn't make sense. I was underneath the Blackwell library...but I wasn't...I mean, I couldn't be.

I lingered, frozen in awe, unable to believe what I was seeing. It was a library, mirroring the one upstairs in a dark and majestic way. Instead of cozy, it was severe. Instead of spooky, it was haunting. Like a dark twin of the Blackwell library.

There didn't seem to be lamps, only a few thick yellow

tapers scattered about the place with flickering magical flames giving off a cold, distant glow. And unlike the Blackwell library, this one had only a handful of bookshelves staggered around the place, shouldered by tall stretches of walls...

The walls.

They were a strange green color that seemed to move, and shifted in odd fluid motions that made my stomach sick. I tried not to look at them. There was a fireplace across the room from where I stood, and the couches and tables were positioned exactly like upstairs. And the place was just as big...but high. It stretched up impossibly high, with several levels of balconies and more bookshelves in between more walls. Blueish-green light poured down from above, glittery bits of aquamarine magic floating down through the air like dust in a sunny room. I looked all the way up at the ceiling, and my mouth fell open.

Sun...I smiled slightly. That's what the light was... sunlight. A glass dome covered the library like the top of a fishbowl, glowing a blueish green. That's when I realized... it was the lake.

This strange library was just barely beneath the surface of the lake.

I rushed forward, the tap of my sneakers on the stone floor echoing through the library. I spun in a slow circle, marveling at the dome, as the golden rays shined on the bright greenery of the mangroves. Then I scoffed at my stupidity. The walls. They weren't walls. They were windows. Tall windows shimmering green with sunlight, plants, water, and an occasional fish. I drifted along the walls and shelves in pensive fascination.

This place was my answer.

But where did I start?

I found the card catalog easily enough. There was an entire drawer dedicated to demons. My stomach lurched uncomfortably as I skimmed the titles. Finally, I managed to find a card with a book title that seemed informative instead of...instructive. I eyed the shelves uneasily. They didn't keep just any old books down here. They kept the dark books. The wicked ones. All the knowledge of a Hallowed House that was too corrupt, too depraved not to keep secret.

And I could *feel* it.

Standing there in the shadowy depths of the place, a dark, twisted power hummed from the tomes arranged neatly in each bookcase. It vibrated against my skin, sending goose bumps up and down my arms.

The books wanted to be opened.

To be used.

I swallowed thickly and tried to fight off my nausea. The kind of spells and curses that lurked inside these books...evil. I shut the catalog drawer, crushing my chosen card slightly in my sweaty hand.

I shouldn't have gone down here.

And I should've left right then.

But I still needed answers.

I studied the card and hurried to find the book. I chewed on my cheek as my eyes scanned the shelves. The books were old and peeling, and the faded titles were dark and frightening. I didn't even want to look at them. Finally, I found the book. I snatched it from the shelf and stuffed it in my bag.

"Well, well, well...what do we have here?"

I flinched, startled. Then I scowled. Great-Aunt Cordelia.

I inhaled sharply and closed my eyes. I gritted my teeth at the annoying taunt of her voice. Awesome.

Slowly, I slid the card inside beside the book, and with barely a movement more, I glided the zipper of my backpack closed. Orange sparkles of magic dusted my fingers.

Cursing myself, I turned to face her with an innocent smile.

She grinned darkly, her potato nose crinkled in the corners. Her eyes glittered in the greenish glow above us. She licked her lips, as though she longed to devour me. "Phoenix Grey...what *have* you gotten into?"

IGNORANCE

She was a hag.

By anyone's standards.

A short, plump woman, Great-Aunt Cordelia was a below-average witch with an above-average ego. She may have been Grammy's sister, but they could not have been more different...and I'm not talking opposites like Seraphina and me. It was like Cordelia Blackwell and Nancy Grey were not even the same *species*. There was something rotten about Cordelia, as though something inside her had gone bad, festering and rank. And as I sat, slouched in the couch cushions of the Blackwell library, I swear I could smell it.

I scrunched up my nose as I continued to grin up at her. She stared back with that same hungry smile on her face, standing rigid in front of Grammy's desk beside the fireplace. The secret entrance had vanished. My backpack was clutched in her hand.

She couldn't open it. I'd had to bite down on my smirk to keep from laughing as she'd struggled with the zipper.

I inclined my head and studied her. It was as if she should've been a bad witch, but was forcing herself to be good...and she stunk at it.

The doors creaked open.

Grammy and Uncle Richard entered the room. Uncle Richard's brow was creased with concern, and Grammy's face was pinched and impassive. I had a sinking feeling that maybe I was in more trouble than even *I* could wiggle out of...

Cordelia's face lit up with eager anticipation as they approached. She thrust my backpack at Grammy. "I caught her sneaking down in the Archives. I can't imagine how she got down there—" She shot me a nasty sneer. "But that's immaterial. She has stolen a book."

Grammy pursed her lips in a tight frown. Her eyebrow raised as she took the heavy bag. Grammy tried the zipper. Her eyes met mine.

I smiled sheepishly and shrugged.

Cordelia's lip curled in disgust as she waved her stubby arm toward me. "Clearly, she put some kind of jinx on the bag!"

Grammy walked over to stand in front of me. She dropped my backpack onto the coffee table beside the mess of books I'd made. "Phoenix...what were you doing down in the Archives? You had to have known those books were off-limits...and potentially dangerous."

"I was looking for answers...the library was just being helpful." I grinned cheekily.

Cordelia lunged forward with a sly smirk. "See, Nancy! This is why you can't homeschool young witches—they end up ignorant and bored...and then they begin experimenting with the dark arts! Making demon deals for more power! We've seen it over and over—"

My eyes flashed. I got to my feet. "Why don't you—"

"Phoenix..." Grammy shook her head. She cleared her throat and waved a hand in my direction. "Please, explain."

I shot Cordelia a scathing glare and then turned to Grammy. I took a deep breath. "I needed answers—"

"See!" Cordelia cackled excitedly. "My, my...another Grey has gone dark—"

I scoffed. "Well, it takes one to know—"

"Cordelia!" Grammy snapped.

I flinched at the sound. I'd never heard her so angry.

Grammy turned to her sister, her face cold and marred with disgust. "That is *enough*," she said coolly.

Cordelia held her tongue, but the look in her eyes as she glared at Grammy said everything. She pursed her lips and then spoke through gritted teeth. "Nancy...the girl has trespassed into the tomes of the Archives. She's stolen a book. *I expect her to be punished.*"

Uncle Richard cleared his throat. The three of us peeked back at him just in time to see the secret entrance seal itself up. He crooked his finger at Grammy, who hurried over to him. She bent her ear down to listen as he whispered something to her. Then Grammy straightened, nodded, and walked back toward us, her head held high.

Uncle Richard winked at me. It was so fast I nearly missed it. A cocky grin slid onto my face. I looked between

Cordelia and Grammy, waiting with a renewed, patient confidence.

"Richard has searched the Archives. The book that was taken is a reference book. Purely educational. I'm sure there's an innocent explanation for her trespass—"

Cordelia's eyes widened in outrage. Her face contorted and her potato nose purpled.

I snickered.

She looked like she might explode.

She blew a raspberry, instead. "Oh, a reference book? *Is that all*?" She threw her hands up in the air. Then Cordelia shook her head, her waist-length grizzly gray braids flying every which way. Her voice was a low snarl, her teeth gnashing nastily as she rounded upon me, her finger pointing in my face. "I know what section she was sniffing about...and I will not sit by while this one summons up a demon for—"

"Enough, Cordelia." Uncle Richard spoke harshly from where he leaned against the mantel. "Why don't we let Phoenix explain herself—*without* interruption..."

I grinned, tilted my chin high, and crossed my arms over my chest. "I'd love to..."

Cordelia shot him a look over her shoulder. "I've had enough of this! If the two of you are willing to turn a blind eye to the obvious—" She blew another raspberry, tossing her braids over her shoulders. "A disrespectful, spoiled brat —even worse than the little feral one. At least Seraphina knows her place...I heard she has finally decided to acclimate to a *normal* lifestyle—"

My smirk slipped. I narrowed my eyes and took a step toward Cordelia.

Cordelia hesitated in the face of my fury. She shut her mouth quickly and then sniffed haughtily. "Well...I agree with you, Nancy. Enough is quite enough. I bid you both a good evening." With that, she stomped from the library, her skirts swishing noisily, as she mumbled loudly under her breath.

Grammy closed her eyes and massaged her temples. "Phoenix Grey...what are we going to do with you?"

"Send me home with a box of those chocolate peanut butter candy cupcakes Fawn keeps bragging about?" I flashed a cheesy grin.

Grammy cocked a dubious eyebrow as she regarded me with pursed lips. "Explain. Now."

I sighed, threw my hands in the air, and slapped them at my sides. "I needed answers. No one tells us anything... and I'm sure you're all under strict orders from Mama to keep us in blissful ignorance—but I heard some things..."

Grammy and Uncle Richard exchanged a glance.

I frowned and continued loudly, "And apparently, my homeschool education has been a bit...lacking in areas. But I think it's important to know about what's going on in the real world...especially when my mother is being called off for secret missions against dark things and devil armies."

Grammy looked at me sharply, her brow furrowed.

I shrugged underneath her scrutiny and blew my bangs out of my face. "Some guy Mama knows showed up at the cottage. He wasn't a witch. He was some kind of monster hunter. He let a few things slip."

Grammy shifted where she stood; her dozens of bracelets sparkled as she crossed her arms. "And I'm sure you didn't try to stop him—I'm sensing a case of mistaken identity?"

I flashed an innocent smile. "You know me..."

Grammy scoffed. "Oh, Phoenix!"

"Well! What would *you* do?" I nodded toward her, knowing full well she wouldn't just sit on her hands. I crossed my arms. "So, tell me—who's the Dark One? And what's going on?"

Grammy and Uncle Richard exchanged another glance, long and pointed.

I jutted my jaw to the side in annoyed impatience. I put my hands on my hips as I watched them.

Grammy inhaled deeply, her nostrils flaring. She turned back to study me carefully. Then she lifted my backpack and easily unzipped the bag, her magic glittering like sparkles of silver. My jinx was no match for her. She broke it without even trying. She pulled out the book, *Demonic Forces: A Guide to Soul Protection*. Her eyes moved over the cover. Then, after a moment, she lowered the book and nodded to the couch.

"Sit."

HEY LOOK MA, I MADE IT

I flinched.

The phone screeched through the silence of the cottage.

I pushed out from the kitchen table and made my way to the phone to check the number. My heart leapt in my chest.

I snatched the phone off the hook and gripped it hard to my ear. "Mama?"

"Hey, sweetheart. How—"

"Are you okay?" I blurted.

"Of course I'm—"

"Why didn't you tell us?"

There was a pause. "Phoenix..."

My heart was in my throat, my voice breathless and high, as I fired off every question that popped into my head. "Why didn't you tell us there were evil things out there? Like demons? And ghosts? And monsters? How could you keep that from us?"

There was silence and then a soft sigh blew into my ear. "Traven told me he'd been a bit too—"

"Honest?" I snapped, squeezing the phone so tight in my hand it hurt. I leaned against the wall, the phone cord wrapping around my stomach. "I went to Blackwell Manor."

Silence.

"I know what you're doing." I swallowed thickly. "I know about the Dark One."

"Phoenix, I need you to keep this to yourself...okay? Do not burden Seraphina with this, please?"

I scoffed in disbelief. "But Mama—"

"I want to explain things to *both* of you when I get back...it's a conversation that perhaps I should've had before I left—but I just...I need you to keep this between us for now. Okay?"

I didn't answer. Instead, I stared moodily at the phone cord as I twirled it around my fingers.

"I know you hate keeping secrets, Nix. But I need you to trust me on this." She took a deep breath. "Please?"

I scrunched up my mouth in a thoughtful pout. "Fine. But as soon as you get back, you explain everything. *Everything.*" I scowled at the empty kitchen. "And when *is* that, by the way?"

She hesitated. "I'm going to be longer than I thought—"

"Because you're fighting Darth Vader?" I quipped. "Or is it Lord Voldemort?"

Mama laughed, and the warm, familiar sound teased a smile from the corner of my mouth. "Oh, Phoenix. I don't know what they told you—but I'll do everything I can to explain things to both of you when I get home."

"Fine," I conceded begrudgingly.

"I don't have much time, so talk to me—how are you?"

Much later that evening, I was sitting at the kitchen table, munching on a bowl of M&Ms, and poring over the only book Grammy had allowed me to leave Blackwell Manor with: *Witchcraft: A History*. It wasn't very helpful, and it was so boring, it took all my willpower not to fall asleep at the table. And okay, I kind of did. Head propped up by my hand, I'd drifted off a bit. Only to be startled awake when Icarus launched himself onto the table.

"Seraphina's home."

My chin slipped from my palm. My eyelids fluttered open. "Huh?"

I saw the glow of the headlights move across the ceiling and then pull away. I snapped the book shut. I flicked my finger at the cabinet under the sink and then waved my hands over the book, sending it floating through the air and sliding neatly between bottles of soap and cleaning supplies. I waved my hand again and the cabinet closed quietly behind it.

I snapped my fingers. After a moment, a thick spell-book floated into the kitchen and dropped in front of me. I popped an M&M into my mouth.

Seraphina came inside the cottage quietly, as though

she hoped I was sleeping. I rolled my eyes and slapped at a page of the book.

She halted awkwardly in the archway at the sight of me. Icarus sat, back straight and green eyes staring right at her.

I didn't bother to look up.

Wordlessly, she hurried to the cabinet.

I hid a smirk, keeping my eyes on the page. No more donuts for Phin. I felt her eyes on me and heard her mumble to herself as she moved around the kitchen.

"You missed Fawn again…" I muttered coolly.

I turned a page with such force it crinkled the paper.

She didn't answer. Instead, she grabbed her plate of crackers and cheese and headed out of the kitchen.

"Mama called," I added dryly.

She froze in the doorway. She backed up and slowly placed her plate down on the table.

I tossed a candy into my mouth and slapped another page.

I could feel her eyes on me as she towered over the table, waiting for me to explain. But I wouldn't. I'd said enough. Her turn. I picked up my pencil and scribbled a note in the margin of the page. I turned to the next one, talking softly to myself, "*The absconditus spell is to hide, and stupefeaciunt to stun…*"

"Well?" she snapped. "What did she say?"

Lazily, I made another note and grabbed another M&M. "She's going to be gone longer than she thought."

"What does that *mean*?" Phin murmured, exasperated.

Her stony, defensive posturing disappeared. "It's been two days already…no, *three*, if you count today!"

I shrugged and popped another candy into my mouth.

"She didn't say anything else? What is she doing? Where is she?" Her voice was strained, breathless with increasing anxiety.

I looked up slowly from the spellbook. I studied her critically and popped several more M&Ms. I wanted to tell her. More than anything. I shoved a handful of M&Ms in my mouth. I had to keep chewing to hold in all I knew. I hated keeping things from her. Even though we were in some weird standoff, she was still my sister. My best friend. I needed to tell her.

"Well?"

But I couldn't.

"She said that's all I could say." I shrugged lazily, hiding my internal struggle as best as I could manage.

"'That's all you could say'?" she demanded. "What the hex does that mean?"

I frowned, my voice rising with my temper. All the anger and frustration I felt at her for leaving me and running off to that stupid school boiled to the surface. "I thought they taught grammar at school? Did you not understand the statement? Or were you just not listening? Mama said *that's all I could tell you.*"

She tossed her head, sending her long blonde hair over her shoulder, and she crossed her arms over her chest. "So, she told you more than that? Why would she tell *you* something and not me?"

I rolled my eyes and blew my black bangs out of my

eyes, the orange tips flickering like fire. "Not everything is about you, Phin."

"Right, because it's always about you!"

I pushed back in my chair and stood, my hands firm on the table to keep from strangling her. "I'm not the one so desperate for attention, I needed to run off to a new school to get it!"

Seraphina's silver eyes flashed. "I'm sorry for making friends without asking your permission!"

Icarus's ears twitched, his tail flicking angrily, as we shouted back and forth.

I scoffed with a cruel smirk. "Just because you met someone once doesn't make them your friend."

Her silver eyes shone with hurt, her stony expression slipping.

Guilt cooled my anger, and I snapped defensively, "I was here when Mama called; it's not my fault you weren't!"

Phin scoffed, recovering quickly. "Jealousy clashes with your dye job, Nix."

My eyes blazed bronze. "Did it ever occur to you that Mama has real, life-and-death issues to deal with, things more important than making the cheerleading squad or—or, you know, getting invites to parties?"

She flinched, stepping back from the table, as though I'd struck her. "You're just jealous," she hissed lamely.

I burst out laughing at the ridiculousness of it all. I shook my head. This was just all so stupid.

Phin tried again. "You're just jealous because I actually have friends now, and you're still *alone*."

I rolled my eyes, still smirking. I had Cole and Rachel. Fawn and Mama. They were enough for me, thanks. "Quality over quantity, Phin."

She hit harder. "You can't stand the fact that I finally got away from you!"

The laughter died slowly on my face.

And there it was.

She'd finally said it aloud.

The real reason she left. To get away from me.

We stared at each other in silence.

My eyes burned.

I sniffed and forced a smile. "You know what...you're right. I'd rather be alone than stuck here with you."

I pushed past her into the living room.

I grabbed my backpack off the hook and yanked the front door open, slamming it behind me with such force the whole cottage shuddered. I marched down our gravel drive and disappeared into the night.

KNOW YOUR ENEMY

Martin Isle, or Nile as we islanders called it, was a strip of island in the middle of Lake Champlain, about twenty miles long but only three miles wide, and most kids, myself included, got around just fine on foot, especially because we knew the island like the back of our hand. Even in the dark.

I hitched my backpack farther up on my shoulders, wishing I'd emptied it first. The giant spellbook, and my hoard of other random things stuffed inside it, felt like a boulder strapped to my back. I shifted the bag up again, wincing underneath the weight. I turned left toward Hyde Road. There wasn't really a question of where to go. Anyone who knew me would know I'd go for the Tracks.

Back when railroads were actually relevant, a train had passed through the heart of Nile, and over a long bridge across the lake to New York. But then cars got faster, trains seemed slower, and the railroad was abandoned in favor of Route 2. The bridge to New York was blown up. The railroad was ripped up from the ground. But unbeknownst to most, there was still a little stretch of track that remained, hidden at the edge of the woods, off Bell Hill Road. The Tracks. They were our secret spot—Seraphina, Cole, Rachel, and I. We liked to think that anyway, though I'm sure at least a few island kids had stumbled upon the place at some point. But not many...the Tracks weren't easy to get to.

After walking halfway down Bell Hill, it took a hop over a culvert, a drop down a ditch, a few jumps across a stream, and a long hike down the grassy remains of the railroad route that cut through the forest, steaming full speed toward the lake. Now the path was a bit overgrown and hidden by the giant trees that stretched up and leaned over, blocking out the sky. After a long walk all the way through the woods, the path reached the cliff that dropped into the lake. The Tracks...but there weren't many *actual* train tracks left. Just enough toward the end to make it hard to find your footing, especially at night.

It was a different kind of darkness inside those woods. But the end was worth it: the path sloped up a bit and emerged from the forest atop a small rocky cliff overlooking the lake and a few of the smaller isles, opening up for all the stars. It was beautiful. My favorite place in the world, and worth a bit of a creepy trek through the trees. But I didn't make the hike just for the view.

The walk itself was therapy. By the end of it, I'd usually sorted out whatever argument Phin and I'd had, and I could go back home with a smile on my face.

And this latest fight was no different. Sure, she was

being a hag, but I understood. It was hard for her. She knew more about magic, more about *everything* than me—well, at least, she *had* before I had to start keeping all these supernatural secrets—and she worked extremely hard to learn it all. But still, no matter how hard she worked, no matter how hard she tried, she couldn't even cast the simplest of spells.

Honestly, it didn't make sense. How could a witch *not* have magic? Mama said it happened sometimes, and it didn't make Seraphina any less of a witch...which sounded nice and all, but none of it would ever change how Phin felt. And if she needed to go off and pretend to be ordinary, I could understand that.

But it *wasn't* about the magic...not really.

And tonight confirmed it.

What she really needed was to be away from me.

To get away from me.

But I could understand that, too, even if it hurt like a hex. Magic meant something different to Seraphina than it did to me. She loved it, she respected it, she used to study it all the time. For me, I couldn't care less about perfecting my craft. I was admittedly an underachiever in the magical studies department...which probably had to do with my guilt, as much as my concern for Phin's feelings. Because for some reason, she took my magical ability as her personal failure. She put an incredible pressure on herself to compete with me...but it's hard to compete when you don't have the tools to participate. And she'd always felt that way—that my success was her failure. So, I never tried to succeed at anything. And no matter what she said, or how much of a hag she acted, I was protective of her. And if she needed me to be her proverbial punching bag—so be it.

But not tonight.

Tonight, I was way too mad to be a martyr.

Scowling and still fuming, I turned off Hyde Road, onto Bell Hill Road. My pace slowed.

A truck was parked on the side of the road. The same truck the hunters drove. I almost turned around. Almost. But I was too angry at Phin to want to go home. And, as much as I hated to admit it, my curiosity was piqued.

Bell Hill Road was avoided by locals. Not many people bothered with it. Legend said the road was haunted. But in Nile, the Most Haunted Town in America, almost every place was...*supposedly*...so, that didn't mean much. And, aside from the path to the Tracks, there wasn't anything on it. No houses—nothing. It was just a long curvy road, cut through the trees, connecting Hyde Road to Martin Road.

I approached the truck cautiously, eyeing the dark woods surrounding the road. The light from the moon, half hidden in the shadow of night, streamed through the tops of the trees, shading the road and surrounding grassy ditches in black and blue.

The truck was off. It didn't look like anyone was inside. Traven said they had a room at the By the Lake Motel...so Logan wouldn't need to sleep in it or anything. He had to be somewhere in the woods.

But why?

I came around the truck bed and lifted onto my tiptoes to see inside.

"See anything you like?"

I leapt away from him. Instinctively, my hand splayed in an aura of flame that illuminated both of our faces. Logan didn't flinch, and instead scowled, squinting into the magic fire. I dropped my hand. The fire vanished along with my fear. I glared up at him in the dark. "What are you doing out here?"

"I could ask you the same thing—if I cared." He wrenched open the truck door and tossed in his rucksack. Then he turned to me, his face bathed in the yellow truck light. "Now, if you're all done snooping, I've got places to be."

I crossed my arms and leaned against the side of the truck.

Logan cocked an eyebrow, and his scowl deepened. "You shouldn't be out here, Grey. Especially not on this road."

"Why? Monsters?" I quipped with a lazy shrug to distract from the slight quiver in my voice.

"Ghosts."

I hesitated, studying him closely. "Are you talking about the—"

"Haunting of Bell Hill Road? Yup."

I considered this, frowning. We were always running up and down Bell Hill to get to the Tracks, and we'd never run into anything...unnatural. I would've heard about it— if not from Cole, then definitely from Rachel. She had a big mouth and even bigger imagination. "It's just a ghost story."

"Exactly." Logan studied me grimly.

I tried not to shift my eyes to the woods. "So—what? You're ghost hunting or something?"

Logan didn't answer.

Before I could stop myself, I asked, "How do you do it?"

Logan scoffed, smirking at the question. "Trust me. You couldn't handle it."

I frowned, insulted. "I bet I'd do a better job than *you*."

He smiled slightly and nodded toward the truck. "Whatever you say. Come on. I'll take you home."

I tilted my chin ever so slightly, irritated by his amusement. "No, thanks. I'll take my chances." I pushed off the truck and continued on my way. Immediately, I was plunged into darkness and weak, waning moonlight. The road I knew so well suddenly felt long and ominous. But I didn't slow down. I'd rather face a ghost than admit to this idiot that I was scared...maybe.

"Grey...just get in the truck."

I turned to face him and continued to walk backward. "Or what?"

"Or I'll have to follow you home," Logan said dryly.

I rolled my eyes. "That's just stupid."

"Agreed. But Traven made it my job to keep an eye on you and your sister. So that's what I'm going to do."

I stopped walking. "You always do what you're told?"

"Yup."

I frowned thoughtfully. "Well, that's not my problem...and your problem isn't me..." I pointed my finger at his back tire. The tire glowed with orange magic dust. "Right now, it seems to be that tire."

Logan slammed his truck door and stomped around to check his truck. "Are you kidding me?"

"Oh, relax. It'll be fine—as long as you don't try to follow me...then it might just...pop." I snickered and turned back around, quickening my pace. My bag bounced hard against my back, the massive spellbook thumping against my spine.

Logan cursed loudly. Then he called after me, "You might want to tell that sister of yours to be careful."

I stopped short, gripping the strap of my backpack tight. I looked over my shoulder to squint at him through the darkness. "What do you mean?"

"I've seen her at that school." Logan, just a black figure leaning against the truck, seemed to shrug. "She plays the good witch part real well. But there's something going on in this town—something evil." He yanked open his door, holding it open for a second. "And if I find out she's gone dark, I won't hesitate to put her down." He slammed the door and revved the engine, blasting me with high beams. Then he pulled onto the road and sped off, leaving me all alone on haunted Bell Hill Road.

* * *

I didn't go to the Tracks.

Instead, I doubled back and hurried home, Logan's words haunting me worse than any ghost possibly could. If bad things were happening, I wanted to make sure

Seraphina had a little extra protection with her—just in case. I crept into our room and slowly slipped around to her side of the bed. The keychains on my backpack knocked together.

Seraphina stirred.

I froze with my face scrunched up, praying she wouldn't wake. She didn't. I let out the breath I'd been holding and slipped my backpack to the floor as quietly as I could manage. Then I slowly unzipped her backpack and tucked one of my charm pouches in the bottom of her bag.

Seraphina let out a little groan.

I froze again, crouched low beside her bed. For a few seconds, I stared at her. She didn't move. Finally, when I was sure she was asleep, I stood in one fluid motion and hopped over to my side of the room. I tossed my wand onto the nightstand and bounced into bed, not bothering to change, and slowly fell into a restless sleep.

I slept late...even for me.

By the time I opened my eyes, golden afternoon sun was pouring into the room from the hallway, and Seraphina was long gone.

I stumbled to my dresser, pulled out some fresh clothes, and changed quickly. Jeans, black *RoadKill* tank top, and a light *Star Wars* hoodie. I smiled. Comfy clothes for the win. I grabbed my wand, tucked it in my topknot, and screwed up my face as I tried to remember where my backpack went.

I snapped my fingers.

Nothing happened.

I flopped onto Seraphina's bed to peek over the side.

Her bag was still there.

Jinx it. She must've taken mine by mistake.

A sly smirk slid onto my face as I jumped to my feet. I hoped she had fun lugging around my stuff all day. My eyes went to her bag. I bit my lip. Should I?

Phin probably wouldn't like it...

I grinned.

Without further hesitation, I yanked her backpack up off the ground and hurried to the kitchen to grab a quick snack.

As I passed the table, I stopped short and smiled. A plate of chocolate peanut butter candy cupcakes sat neatly in the middle of the table with a note that read:

> Nix,
> Grammy said you'd like these.
> Fawn
> PS: Your snores sound like Smaug

I grinned and grabbed a cupcake. They were decadent. A treat for the eyes as much as the tongue: moist chocolate cake with peanut butter frosting, topped with peanut butter cups. Fawn's favorite. I took a big bite. Delicious. I closed my eyes, savoring the sweet, sugary goodness. I finished it in three bites, licking the frosting from my fingertips. Then I dug a to-go box out of the pantry and filled it with a few of them. I tucked the box into a brown paper bag and scrunched it shut.

But would there be room? I slammed Phin's backpack onto the kitchen table and peeked inside. It was stuffed. And heavy. Too heavy. Although, not as heavy as mine. I smirked. Then, without a twinge of guilt, I dumped her school stuff out onto the table and tucked my bag of cupcakes carefully inside.

I glanced at the mess of papers and books and folders all over the place. I looked at the clock. It was late. I'd clean it up later. I tossed the backpack over my shoulder and headed out the door to get some more answers.

8

____

1985

First stop?

Library.

Or rather, Nile's sad excuse for one.

It originally had been the town's one-room school-house. Then, when those went out of style, they added bookcases, stuffed it full of books, and called it a library.

The librarian was a hunched-over, miserable, old crone of a woman, who I strongly suspected hated books. There was no other excuse for the way she kept the place. The tiny room was like a hoarder's den, but in place of garbage —books. Dusty, discarded books stuffed the shelves near to bursting. And the books that couldn't be wedged onto the shelves were stuffed carelessly everywhere else. Stacks littered the floor like rundown skyscrapers. Mounds of books blocked the tiny aisles and made movement nearly impossible. Even the small rectangular windows that lined the ceiling were almost completely blocked by books.

No one stayed in the place for long. Not only was it

impossible to move in there—it was even harder to breathe. I don't know whether it was the librarian, or the library itself, but it stank.

Like farts.

I scooted sideways through the small space between the stacks and shelves to the banker box full of newspapers. I kicked a stool closer to the box and took a seat. The papers were dusty, but at least they were there. I skimmed through the headlines of the *Nile Days* from the past few weeks, searching for anything unusual. Or evil, as Logan had said.

I didn't have to look hard.

There'd been a double murder last week. Sarah and Kyle Rousseau, a married couple. Their throats were ripped open so deep, pieces of their spine were visible. The woman's heart was missing. The doors were locked from the inside. No signs of forced entry.

I glanced up over the mountain of books. The librarian wasn't looking. I couldn't even see her. I folded the newspaper and tucked it into the backpack.

I went back to the papers. Nothing else stood out—except for a car accident...*on Bell Hill Road*. I paused, chewing on my tongue, as I studied the article. The driver, Maddison Rose, 16, said she'd seen a man standing in the middle of the road. But at first glance, she'd thought it was a wolf. She'd swerved straight into a tree. Her sister, Grace-lynn Rose, 9, was in critical condition at Ethan Allen Hospital. I did a double take, shaking out the newspaper. She'd thought it was a wolf...standing?

I craned my neck over the books. Coast was clear. I

folded the newspaper, sliding it in the bag beside the first. Then I stood quickly and weaved my way toward the card catalog. Nothing was in order. I scowled, my eyes sliding over to the librarian. Her messy gray mullet trailed down her back as she hunched like a warty old toad an inch from the computer screen. She had a sour disposition that'd put Aunt Cordelia to shame, but the worst part—she moved slower than death.

I sighed moodily and side-stepped to the front of the desk.

"Excuse me, ma'am?" I forced a bright smile.

The woman turned slowly in her seat. She raised a bushy eyebrow as she blinked at me, her thick glasses magnifying her beady eyes.

She didn't speak.

My smile stretched awkwardly across my face. "Uh— do you happen to have any books on ghosts?"

Her lip curled, as she inclined her head. "Shouldn't you be in *school*?" she asked in a croaky voice through fuzzy yellow teeth.

My smile vanished. I gave her a deadpan stare. "Nope."

She laughed—at least, I think that's what the wheezing sound crackling out of her thick throat was...maybe she was dying.

The stink of her breath engulfed me. I scrunched up my nose.

"Try the card catalog." She nodded in the general direction of the drawers and coughed, wet and hacking, into her palm. She cleared her throat and took a dirty paper towel and dabbed her mouth. "In case you didn't notice—we're *understaffed*. Things are sometimes hard to find. Books on ghosts aren't that popular." She sat up a bit in her chair to peek over the desk littered with junk, papers, and a few books. "You could always look for yourself."

I shook my head in disgusted disbelief. "What about books on Nile...like Nile's history? You have any idea where *they* might be in all this mess?" I waved my hand around the hoard threatening to cave in on us at any moment.

The woman narrowed her eyes. Her gray tongue slid over her crusty lips. "There's a historical society for that, isn't there?"

She turned slowly in her chair, like a toad on a lily pad, and stuck her face back into the computer screen.

I scoffed. "Okay, then."

I turned to leave, pausing behind a bookshelf to peek back at her. Then I pursed my lips into a thoughtful pout, pointed my finger through the shelves, and whispered, "*Varus varius varicella.*"

A slow smile slid onto my face as I watched the woman reach down to scratch her belly. I nodded, grinning with smug satisfaction, and slipped quietly out of the library.

I stopped at Kip's Snack Bar for an early dinner.

It was on the way—and honestly, even if it wasn't...the food was too good to pass up on a road trip...however short. I grabbed an empty picnic table, plopped my tray down, and pulled out the newspaper about Bell Hill Road. And, in between bites of my burger and fries, I combed through the article looking for any hint the accident was paranormal...aside from the standing wolf.

I took out my cupcakes and munched them one by one. Now that I thought about it—there might have been a car accident on Bell Hill Road last year...I couldn't remember. I licked the frosting off my thumb. Nile was such a small town...when things happened, they stood out. I shrugged, tucked the newspaper back in the backpack, and tossed my trash.

By the time I pulled into the circular, looping drive in front of the Martin Isle Historical Society, the sun was low, red and burning just above the trees across the fields at my back. The sky behind the old colonial estate was bruised purple, streaked with low black clouds. An ancient gray tree looming off to the side of the property like a gnarled claw shook slightly in the wind. The old building itself was pushed back from the highway, nestled in a semicircle of woods at its back. And it was huge, white with black shutters, stacked three stories high, with two smoking chimneys on opposite ends at the top, and a large, covered porch wrapping around the base. There was a spooky, ominous air about the place that made me pause, my hand on the car door.

I inhaled deeply, the cool air sharp in my nose. My itch for answers was too strong to stop now. I slammed the door, pocketed the keys, and swung the backpack over my shoulder. I headed up the long stone path and up the steps to the front doors. I pulled open the right one, a small brass bell chiming my arrival.

I smiled as I slipped inside, enveloped in the cozy warmth of the foyer. Inside it was a completely different house. The cream-colored walls and antique oak furniture and fixtures gave off a cheery, homey feel that put me instantly at ease. Like a bed-and-breakfast or something. I crossed my arms and stepped farther inside, my eyes moving over the scenic paintings and grand sweeping staircase.

A tall, lithe, old woman, with wavy, silver hair tied back by scarves, floated into the foyer. Her paisley patterned dress billowed about her as she moved toward me, her arms open, and a bright smile to match her amber eyes. "Welcome to the Martin Isle Historical Society...I'm Zan. How can I help you, dear?"

"Hi—uh, I was interested in anything you could tell me about Bell Hill Road."

Zan's eyes glittered as she looked down her hooked nose at me. "Ahh, a ghost enthusiast...follow me."

She led me up the grand staircase, making occasional comments on the paintings we passed and the history of the house itself. Then she turned down a hall and cut into a side room. It originally had been a guest bedroom of some kind, but now it was an exhibit of local lore with different displays stationed around the perimeter of the room and a giant table in the center.

"This is the Hall of Mysteries. The largest collection of

artifacts relating to the myths and legends of Martin Isle... we are known as the Most Haunted Town in America for a reason, after all." Zan ushered me into the room. "Tell me, dear, what have you heard about Bell Hill Road?"

I shrugged. "Not much. Just that it's supposed to be haunted."

Zan waved her arm toward a large display table in the center of the room. It looked like one of those train set towns people set up in their basements. But there was no train—not anymore. It was clearly a miniature replica of Nile, with Route 2 snaking through the middle of the farm fields, forests, and rolling hills. It didn't have every house and every farm in Nile, only the landmarks and the notable places. The detail was charming, like an elaborate dollhouse. There were even tiny ferry boats floating in a dry Lake Champlain beside the east and west ferry docks.

Zan pointed around the model town as she named a few landmarks. "Nile has many legends...many hauntings... Bird Island...the haunted mirror of the Rosecrest House... the creepy Cow Man...the Wicked Witch Down Old Grey Lane...but Bell Hill Road is one of the saddest legends we have—"

"Why's that?"

Zan gave me a rueful smile as she waved me toward a back corner of the room. "Legends are often stories we tell each other to explain unexplainable things. And the Bell Hill Haunting was born out of a need to explain unexplainable tragedies. Look here."

Zan stopped in front of an old black-and-white photo positioned on a side table. "This is the first recorded car accident on Bell Hill Road after the first reported sighting of the Bell Hill Wolfman."

I picked up the photograph. It was a small Jeep flipped upside down in a ditch. I inclined my head. It was near the culvert...close to the Tracks.

"On October 10th, a young man by the name of Frank Rose was driving home just after dark when he saw a large, black creature lunge at his car from the woods. He swerved and flipped his Jeep. To this day, decades later, he is convinced it was a creature. He also cites the disappearance of Catherine Barrow as further proof of this monster...for while young Catherine Barrow didn't crash her car, it was found abandoned on Bell Hill Road, October 11th of the following year. Now, some...most...have a different theory..."

I put down the photograph and glanced at Zan. "Which is?"

She smiled, her golden eyes sparkling with mischief. "Some say it's not a creature, but a ghost that haunts the road. Here—" Zan moved over to the side and nodded toward a framed newspaper clipping. Her face fell a bit as she studied the paper. She cleared her throat. "Several years after Mr. Rose's encounter, on a late night in early October, a married couple were driving down Bell Hill in a rainstorm. They had gotten lost on their way to the Charlebois Inn...the husband swore he saw *something* standing in the middle of the road. He didn't swerve in time. Says the car went right through it before their car skidded and crashed into a tree." Zan's voice softened a bit as she added, "The wife didn't make it."

My stomach twisted uncomfortably as I stared at the black-and-white image of the car's tires in the air.

"What do *you* think it is, Zan?"

Zan shrugged with a sad smile. "Who can say? Whatever it is, there have been twenty-two car accidents in the first few weeks of October since 1985, so something is on that road...whether ghost or corporeal creature..." She shook head.

I cocked an eyebrow. "If you had to guess?"

Zan thought for a moment. "I'd say ghost...if it was a creature, I'd expect there to be...well—" She made a face. "Body parts, rather than car accidents. And although Miss Barrow did vanish on the road...she is the only disappearance on record after all these years. The only anomaly. And in addition to this, the sightings only appear during the first eleven days of October. After the eleventh day, the sightings stop until the next year. That speaks to symbolic emotional significance, rather than some kind of hibernation period."

Tonight was October 11th. "And how do you stop a ghost? Like...put it to rest?"

Zan bit her lip on her smile. "I think you have 'historian' confused with 'paranormal investigator,' my dear."

I swung the backpack in front of me and pulled out the stolen newspaper with the car accident headline. "Please?"

Zan bit her lip and took the paper gently in both hands. "The Rose girls...Frank Rose is their uncle...I didn't realize they'd been on Bell Hill when—" She clucked her tongue against her teeth. "I'm by no means an expert, Miss

Grey...you'd best ask your mother these questions...hmm?"

I blinked, taken aback at being recognized so easily. I tried to smile, but only managed a wince.

She handed me the newspaper with a warm smile. "She actually helped my grandson and his girlfriend with a ghost a few weeks back..."

I gripped the newspaper, crushing it slightly in my hands. Mama had helped some random Nile kids with a ghost? Unbelievable. I scoffed under my breath and shook my head. I cleared my throat, then folded the paper and slid it back in the bag. I flashed my sweetest smile. "Please, Zan—I'm just trying to understand...and my mom is Unreachable—uhh, you know, *unavailable* at the moment."

Zan inclined her head, smiling indulgently. "A ghost is an unnatural thing. Impure. It can be repelled by that which *is* pure—salt, lavender, and iron are the most common."

"And how would you get rid of it? Like, for good?"

"A ghost is simply a human soul trapped on Earth. To be rid of the spirit, you need to free it from whatever binds it here, be it object or unresolved emotion. Don't ask me how—" Zan held up a finger, her rings shining in the light.

"Unresolved emotion?" I scrunched up my face. "Like unfinished business?"

The doorbell chimed from downstairs.

I flinched and smiled sheepishly, shoving my hands in my jean pockets.

Zan glanced quickly at the door before flashing me a

kind smile. She waved her hand at the books on a large shelf beside the Bell Hill Road display. "Please, help yourself. I'll be around if you need me." Then she gingerly touched my shoulder. "And be careful, Miss Grey. Ghosts can be very vicious beings…"

I smiled as I watched her go. It was nice to have an adult actually be helpful for once. I ran my finger along the weathered spines, my head inclined sideways to read the faded titles. My eyes narrowed curiously as I pulled out a book. A lot of these books were written by the same woman…Rosalind Grunberg.

The floor creaked behind me.

I turned sharply and groaned. Great.

I shoved the book back on the shelf. "What are you doing here, DeVarney?"

He leaned against the doorway, his arms crossed over his chest and a cocky smirk on his face. "I could ask you the same thing—"

"If you cared?" I mocked, rolling my eyes.

Logan jutted his chin toward the model Nile between us. "You're here about Bell Hill, aren't you?"

I scowled and crossed my arms.

Logan rubbed the back of his neck. "God, Grey…you barely have your eyes open, and now you think you can hunt the Bell Hill Road ghost?"

The skepticism in his voice—the way he asked it—rubbed me like sandpaper. It irritated me and made my skin itch. I shoved my fists into my hips. "So what if I am?"

Logan scoffed, shaking his head as he massaged his forehead. "Listen—you can't—"

"I *can't?*" I snorted.

Logan's jaw tightened. He closed the distance between us just so he could tower over me. The giant.

I looked up at him, my face hard and unflinching.

"Hunting monsters—hunting ghosts—it's not a game, okay? It's serious, hard work. And people tend to get hurt. So, no, Nancy Drew. You can't. Go back home to your safe little cottage and stay there. Keep brewing your potions and playing with your spells, or whatever you do all day, and forget you ever heard about any of this."

I wanted to hex him.

Real bad.

I gritted my teeth. My temper boiled over. "Let's get something straight: if I want to catch this ghost—"

"Hunt." Logan nodded with sarcastic seriousness.

"What?" I snapped, exasperated.

"If you want to *hunt* the ghost...you hunt evil—you don't fish for it." Logan grinned, crossing his arms across his broad chest.

"Whatever!" I rolled my eyes. "The point is: if I want to hunt the—the *tooth fairy*, I'll hunt it! Okay? And no—" I stumbled over my retort, gesturing vaguely up and down the length of him. "You know...no flannel-wearing, overgrown *Chewbacca* is going to stop me."

I pushed past him, cheeks burning. I hurried out of the room, down the stairs, and out of the historical society, wishing I'd just kept my mouth shut and hexed him like I'd wanted to in the first place.

9

DONTTRUSTHER

When I got back to the cottage, it was dark.

And Seraphina still wasn't home.

I slammed the door. The cottage shuddered. I was angry. Angry at Logan. Angry at Seraphina. Angry at Mama. Everyone.

I stomped into the kitchen, glaring at the mess of Phin's school stuff I'd left all over the table. Where was she? What could she *possibly* be doing? Suddenly I felt...less than for being at home. Like there was something wrong with me.

I was always at home. That was my life. And I'd always been happy with it. But Seraphina was off, clearly doing things...not that they could be anything I wanted to be doing—but still.

I thought of Logan. Hunting evil. Making the world a safer place. Now *that* sounded like something I'd like to do. I looked around the quiet kitchen. For the first time, I felt inadequate. Like my life was lacking...and definitely *not* for the first time, I felt completely alone.

My eyes burned, and I rubbed them with the heel of my palm. Then I sniffed and got to work. I slapped Seraphina's backpack onto the table and pulled out the newspapers, slipping them discreetly between the spice racks. Then I shoved Seraphina's stuff back inside her bag. I repacked the books, followed by the folders, hesitating on a welcome folder for Mater Christi High School.

Icarus lurked in the doorway, watching me rifling through her things. "Seraphina won't be happy."

Ignoring the cat, I peeked inside the folder.

My heart sank into my stomach.

Crushing the folder in my hand, I slapped it hard on the table. I snatched her bag and dumped it out again, all over the table, even messier than before, then I stalked to the back door. Icarus bolted out of the way just as the back door burst open in an explosion of orange dust. I stomped outside into the night. The door slammed magically behind me.

I ripped my wand out of my hair and pointed it at the empty fire pit as I crossed the grass. "*Incaendium!*"

With a bang, fire shot from the end of my wand and blasted into the pit. My eyes blurred as my blood burned, and I shot again and again.

By the time the moon was high in the inky purple sky, illuminating the fields in the distance, and casting Grey Cottage and the surrounding woods in shadow, I'd perfected my wand work with the spell to the point I could cast it wordlessly.

There was a shout from the depths of the cottage, puncturing the silent night.

The back door banged open.

I squinted into the bright kitchen light that surrounded Seraphina like an aura.

"Surprised you came back," I said coolly, my eyes back on the fire pit.

I shot another burst of fire into the pit.

Seraphina pointed at the back door. "What in the hex did you do to my stuff?!"

I didn't answer.

I fired another shot into the pit and smirked as she flinched.

"Unlike you, I actually have homework, Phoenix! Projects, exams, essays to do! I have important stuff in there!"

I looked up, my eyes glittered in the dark. "You sure wouldn't want to lose all those boarding forms you've collected."

"What?" Phin snapped.

I stabbed my wand through my topknot and stomped back across the grass and up the steps, knocking into her on my way to the kitchen. I snatched up the stack of papers from the table and threw it at her with more magic than I'd intended. The stack burst apart in her face, papers floating through the air.

"Too bad Mama's not here to sign these."

"You don't have any right to go through my stuff," Seraphina muttered as the permission slips fell all around us.

"Were you even going to tell me?" I demanded, my heart pounding, panicked, in my chest. "Or was your plan to have Grammy sign it and just not come back at all?"

"You know, you really need to stop nosing into other people's business, Phoenix. Your little ear-to-the-keyhole habit is going to get you into trouble one of these days."

I shook my head with a sneer. "That's not an answer."

Seraphina threw up her hands. "For Fay's sake, Phoenix! I wasn't going to board, okay? There was a mix-up at the office and the woman gave me some just in case."

"Don't try to tell me you didn't think about it..." My eyes burned with her betrayal. She left me. *Because* of me. She could try to deny it all she wanted, but the truth was evident. She'd rather be anywhere but stuck home with me.

Seraphina forced a laugh. "Fine. I did think about it. I've thought about it all week. But I wasn't going to even *bother* asking."

"Why not?" I challenged.

"You think Mama or Grammy would let me leave poor, precious Phoenix alone? Fay forbid I'm not here to hold your hand!"

I held my head high. "I don't need anyone around me who doesn't want to be."

"Well, I guess that explains why you're alone all day," she quipped nastily.

I flinched, as though she'd smacked me.

Seraphina's stony expression faltered.

I shook my head, my trembling lip curled in disgust. "You know what, go ahead...I don't care anymore."

I crooked my finger and a form lifted from the ground. I caught it in my hand. Then I slid my thumb across the page, leaving a trail of orange glitter. I placed it gently on the table. Mama's signature was looped neatly on the paper in blood-red ink. "There."

Seraphina hesitated, as though torn between snatching up the paper and taking back everything she'd said...but I didn't care.

I snapped my fingers. All the permission slips fluttered through the air, stacking themselves neatly on the table, the paper with Mama's signature on top. Then her books and notebooks tucked themselves tidily back into her backpack and the zipper slid shut with a sparkle of orange magic.

Then, without a word, I walked out of the kitchen.

Seraphina appeared in the doorway just as I threw open the door.

"Where are you going?" she demanded, her voice watery with emotion.

"Don't pretend to care now, Seraphina." I slammed the door behind me.

I told myself I was headed for the Tracks...and if I happened to run into Logan on Bell Hill Road, that wasn't my fault.

But, honestly, I hoped I would.

According to Zan, it was the last night to see the ghost until next year. He'd be there. He had to be.

The road was a long one, a stretch of more than a mile through dense forest with trees that bent overhead like a tunnel. I didn't have to go the entire length of Bell Hill to reach the start of the Tracks...the culvert and the stream leading to the old railroad route were just past the halfway point, but that was more than enough time to get just a bit creeped out by the idea of a ghost lurking somewhere in the dark.

As the road began to bend, my pace quickened. My eyes scanned the tree line just beyond the ditch. I shivered in the cold, cursing myself for not grabbing a heavier jacket. I zipped up my thin *Star Wars* hoodie all the way to my chin and pulled the sleeves down, gripping them tightly in my fists to keep out the chill. I squinted a bit ahead of me, farther up the road.

There was no truck in sight.

I kicked the grass at the side of the road. Jinx it. I would've liked to hunt down a ghost.

My ears prickled.

I turned sharply toward the opposite side of the road. I could've sworn I'd heard something, but there was nothing there...at least nothing that I could make out in the blue-black light of the waning moon.

I kept walking. Fast. I was almost to the culvert. I could hear the soft bubbling of the water below as it drained into the ditch and the gentle trickle of the stream leaking into the woods. I picked up speed. My calves were burning by the time I reached the culvert. But before I could jump down into the ditch, there was a flash of headlights at my back. Then a sound screeched through the silence that made my arms prickle and shoulders hunch.

The scream of tires on the asphalt.

JUST THE GIRL

I flinched as the squeal echoed through the night and braced myself for a crash. An impact. But there was nothing. I turned on my heel and ran back down the road toward the headlights. It was a small minivan and inside, in the glow of the radio, I could see the driver was a girl, who couldn't have been older than me. She was staring wide eyed, straight ahead of her, as though there was something there...or had been. Then she blinked as I ran through her high beams, watching me as I came up to her window. She slapped the lock button on the car which thumped quickly into place. I knocked on the window and shouted through the glass. "Are you okay? What happened?"

She looked at me sideways, as though she were afraid to make eye contact with me. And I couldn't blame her. I would be freaked out, too, if some girl jumped at my window in the middle of the night...especially if I'd just seen a ghost. I shot a quick glance toward the road and then tapped on the glass. "Hey...my name is Phoenix. You shouldn't be out here...not on this road."

At that, the girl turned to face me, her dark round eyes black in the shadow of the minivan. She swallowed hard. Then she switched off the engine and unlocked the van. I stepped back, and she got out. She shut the door. She shivered in the cold and pulled her *X-Men* hoodie tight around her. "Are you here because of the ghost, too?"

I hesitated.

The girl blinked, her sad eyes shining in the moonlight. She scoffed with a rueful smirk and a shake of her head. "I had to see it again...to convince myself I wasn't crazy...but I probably am—"

"You saw the ghost?" I demanded, my voice thin. I looked down the road and then back at her.

She rocked back and forth on her heels and nodded slowly. A cold gust of October wind blew past us, catching her thick dark hair and swirling it around her heart-shaped face. She tucked it back behind her ears. "I saw it last week...my sister and I...our uncle always said it was a monster. You know how old islanders like to talk..." She shook her head again, her teeth biting down on her trembling lip. Her voice dropped to a harsh whisper, "But I was so sure it was a ghost."

Her uncle. I swung my backpack around, pawing at the pockets. I yanked out the newspaper, as though I might see the headline in the dark. "Are you Gracelynn Rose?" I blurted quickly, struggling to remember the names of the girls in the car accident last week. I held out the paper for her, but she didn't move to take it. She inhaled sharply. But before she could answer, headlights turned onto the road. The both of us flinched, shuffling closer together. The truck swerved around us, barreling down the road so fast he could've been drag racing. The rush of air blew past us, catching our hair and whipping it around our faces. There was a beep in her pocket, and she fumbled for her phone. She checked the message, and her face fell. Then, as though she just realized we were standing in the middle of the road, she yanked the van door open. Then she paused and turned back to me. "Do you need a ride? I need to get home...I'm not even supposed to have the car." She sniffed. "I don't know what I was thinking coming back out here."

"Did you see him?" I grabbed the doorframe, keeping her from shutting it. "Just now?"

She winced and hopped inside the van. "No," she murmured sadly. "It's just another Nile legend. I didn't see it last week. And I didn't see it tonight." She put her hand on the handle and met my gaze. "And you're right. I shouldn't be out here. And neither should you. Do you want a ride?"

I stepped back with a small smile, squinting into the glare of the van light. "I'll be okay."

The girl gave me a weak smile as I gently shut her door and backed up toward the opposite side of the road. She cranked the engine, and her headlights snapped on. I blinked hard. I could've sworn I saw something. But there was nothing. And I watched as she turned the van in a tight semi circle and drove back the way she'd come, leaving me alone on the moonlit road.

I took a deep, shaky breath. Maybe she was right. It wasn't like Logan was out here anyway. I headed down the road toward home and away from the Tracks.

But, I didn't get far.

I squinted into the darkness. My pace slowed. There was something big in the road ahead of me. I stopped, frozen on the yellow lines. I didn't dare leave the road...I didn't know these woods, especially not at night. I'd get lost until morning.

I blinked.

Whatever shadow I'd seen was gone. I exhaled deeply, my breath clouding hot in my face.

There was a sound heading toward me. A steady, rhythmic, panting sound. Like something running. I turned sharply and tore down the street back the way I'd come, toward the culvert and the Tracks, as fast as I could. I panted, wincing at the stitch in my side. It haunted the road. Maybe I'd be safe if I made it to the Tracks.

I kept running. I had to be close to the stream...I was sure of it...but I was wrong.

I wasn't close.

I was there.

Running full speed, I missed the ditch, pitching forward into the darkness.

I scrambled to my feet, cold and wet and sore. Something giant stood on the other side of the water, the half-moon high in the sky casting it in shadow. I pulled my wand slowly from my hair and pointed it at the shadow man.

Then it started to laugh.

I blinked stupidly, heart hammering loudly in my ears.

A flashlight clicked on.

I winced, squeezing my eyes shut. The light was blinding.

"Grey, is that you?"

I gritted my teeth.

Logan.

Sticking my wand back into my hair, I held up my hand to shield my face from the spotlight. "Can you not?" I snapped, scowling with squinted eyes.

"Whatever you say, Grey..." Logan lowered the light, his face cracked in a sly smirk. "Was that you I saw chit-chatting with the soccer mom?"

"Something just chased me down the road—" I clutched my side, trying to catch my breath. I narrowed my eyes as I registered his question. "I thought I recognized that old beater of yours. You drive like a maniac!"

Logan shrugged. "I had to...I heard the tires squeal. It was just a matter of time before he went after Soccer Mom."

"That girl was—" I pointed back up toward the road. My heart stalled in my chest. Something stood on the embankment right above me.

"OI!" I whipped out my wand, pointed it at the thing, and sent a jet of fire at it. It disappeared before the spell hit. But I'd seen it in the firelight. My breath escaped me in a low hiss.

Logan sloshed through the stream, not bothering with the hopping stones. "What'd you see?"

"It was—" I blinked rapidly, trying to focus, to process

what exactly I'd seen. It was a guy...but his face was—wrong: snarling, with dead, glassy eyes...covered with matted fur like—

I stabbed my wand back through my topknot just as Logan grabbed my arm and pulled me into him. He held up a crowbar in front of us like a sword. "We need to move. Now."

I scoffed and elbowed him off me. "I can walk just fine on my own, thanks."

Logan nudged me forward. "Then move."

"Do you have any kind of plan?" I snapped back as we hiked up the steep incline onto the road.

Logan rolled his eyes in impatience. "I did, until Soccer Mom had to go and rile him up."

I eyed the dark woods that surrounded us. "What was it? Like a werewolf?"

"It's a ghost," Logan said dryly.

"The ghost of a monster?" I quipped dubiously.

Logan scowled. "No, not— *Look out!*"

The thing appeared beside me, its gnarled face leering with a wide, insane smile that shone in the moonlight.

Logan swung at it with a crowbar. It was too fast. The crowbar only swiped through air. It reappeared beside us. Logan tried to yank me away, but it slashed out with hands curved like claws, with such force it ripped at my skin, tearing thick gashes into my arm. I gritted my teeth on a scream.

Logan swung again. The thing vanished before he could hit it.

"Move." Logan dragged me down the street.

Panting and cradling my mangled arm, I wrestled my other out of his grasp. "Talk."

We moved quickly up the road, casting glances over our shoulders to make sure it wasn't following us.

"Don't you know the story of Bell Hill Road?" Logan snapped, breathless and impatient. "You were just talking with Zan today, for—"

"Obviously!" I snapped back. "After dark, a monster jumps out at cars and—"

Logan scoffed. "No, that's not—"

I groaned. "Oh, for Fay's sake! Get to the point!"

"Fine!"

I could just barely make out the shadow of Logan's truck. I walked faster.

"Every year during the first eleven days of October, Bell Hill is haunted by the ghost of—"

"A wolfman?"

Logan shook his head, muttering furiously to himself. We reached the truck and stopped short. He pulled down the tailgate. Then he dug through a rucksack in the back and passed me a crowbar to match his.

"Iron. The ghost comes at you? Swing. Hard." He tossed his ruck over his back and shut the tailgate.

I winced as my arm throbbed and gripped the cold metal like a club. I shivered in the cold. My teeth chattered slightly.

"Hey...how's that arm?"

My breath came in a cloud in front of my face. I opened my mouth to answer, but I sucked the words back in as the ghost appeared beside him. "Logan!"

With a vicious hiss that stopped my heart, the ghost lunged at him. Logan sidestepped as the ghost slashed at his arm with a blue-white hand. The ghost's fingers clamped down on him and squeezed. I swung the crowbar at him. Just like Logan, I missed; the ghost disappeared before I could connect.

"Grey, behind!" Logan bellowed. He rushed forward with his crowbar high. I whirled around. The ghost appeared in front of me. I jumped to the side as Logan swung hard. In a burst of icy cloud, it exploded in my face. I gasped for air, my eyes darting all around. My chest heaved up and down with my labored breath. Adrenaline pumped through me. My muscles twitched.

Logan let his crowbar fall. He turned to me. "Okay, we need to—"

I wasn't listening. I was watching the woods. I turned sharply toward the right, freezing in place, afraid to move. I tucked my hair behind my ears and stared into the woods. Then I looked at Logan, my eyes wide and shining in the moonlight. "Did you hear that?"

Logan blinked, glancing quickly at the trees. "No—"

"I thought I heard someone calling from the woods..." I looked at Logan uncertainly.

He shook his head. "There wasn't any noise—"

I flinched again, my eyes darting to the woods. "Are you sure?"

I strained my ears. Only the ruffle of a shallow breeze through the leaves answered. I shifted my feet, my grip tightening on the crowbar, cold in my hand. "I thought I heard—"

"Grey..."

Seraphina. My eyes darted to Logan.

Logan stepped in front of my vision, blocking me from the woods. "It's trying to lure you off the road. To separate us." His voice was steady and calm as he said slowly, "Do not get off this road."

But before I could stop myself, I stepped toward the woods.

WASTING TIME WITH YOU

Logan cut in front of me and grabbed my shoulder. Hard. He squeezed so tight I cried out. I stared, eyes wide in shock, frozen for a moment. Then I jolted myself out of it, and I turned to Logan. "I don't know what I was thinking—"

"I told you. Don't go in the woods." Logan hitched his bag higher on his shoulder. "Come on."

I sputtered after him as he marched back down the road in the direction of the Tracks. I glanced toward the woodline. "I thought this thing haunted the road! Why would it want us to go into the woods?"

Logan didn't answer.

I hurried after him, struggling to keep up. I winced at the cramp in my side, my calves burning and my lungs heaving. "You—want—to explain?"

His steps were like two of mine. He was so tall, and I was so...not. I was jogging to keep up with his rapid hike down the road.

"Logan!" I snatched at his arm and pulled him to a stop. "We have to take care of this ghost, and if I'm going to help you, you need to explain!"

He shook himself free. "No, Grey. *I* have to take care of it. You can go home."

"What?" I sputtered. "I'm helping! I—"

"Then help." Logan shrugged and continued to march down the road. "Come on."

I groaned angrily and charged after him. "You have to start talking. Help me understand."

We got to the culvert. Logan hopped down into the ditch, the flashlight beaming back and forth over the stream.

I followed him, slipping just a bit on the cold, grassy embankment. "Well?"

He dropped his rucksack at my feet. "All right, take this—" Logan slapped the flashlight in my hand. "And point it at the stream."

My jaw jutted to the side, and I gritted my teeth. "That doesn't explain—"

"Bell Hill Road is haunted." Logan waded into the water. "By a ghost—not a monster."

"If it's a ghost, how could it grab us?" I snapped impatiently as I tried to follow his movements with the flashlight. "And why does he look like the wolfman?"

Logan ignored my questions. "Back on October 1st, 1985, a kid and his buddies decided to pull a prank on the town. Connor McCallum dressed up in a wolfman mask, and they all hid down in this ditch and waited for a car to come." Logan felt around in the water, swinging his boots side to side under the slow flow of the stream. "Then Connor jumped out and scared the car. They thought it was funny, so they kept doing it. Made the prank a nightly thing, keeping it a secret, hoping it'd become another Nile legend. Then one night, it went wrong. Frank Rose flipped his jeep. McCallum should've taken that as a warning. But, he didn't. The next night, Connor jumped out, and the car hit him before it could swerve...and now his ghost haunts the road every year, on the first few nights of October leading up until the anniversary of his death, October 11th, crashing as many cars as he can until midnight..."

I pointed the light into Logan's face. "And after midnight?"

Logan sneered in the harsh light. I dropped the beam back to the water, a small smirk at my lips.

"And after midnight—" Logan continued gruffly. "He disappears until next year...which is why we only have so many hours to get this done."

"Wow. You sure wait until the last minute," I quipped dryly. "And I thought I had procrastination problems..."

Logan scowled into the light. "You know, there's more to solving a case of paranormal activity than just showing up to kill something. You have to research, interview locals, figure out what you're dealing with...it takes time."

I was only half listening to him. "So, we have to find what his ghost is tied to..." I muttered to myself.

Logan snorted at that. "What do you think I'm doing? Trying to clean my boots?"

I shook my head. This still didn't seem right. "But, why would he want us to leave the road?"

"I told you. To separate us. Chances are, he knows what we're up to…" He continued wading through the stream, boots nudging the bottom. Then he bent over and reached his hands in the water, waving them side to side. "Connor's mom told me his buddies had some geeky, Viking funeral for him at this stream. They sank his— aha." Logan's hands stopped searching. "Got it. Finally." He scoffed. "I've been looking for this thing all night."

He pulled out a rectangular box from the depths of the stream and headed toward the bank to drop it at my feet. "If he's tied to anything, his mom said it'd be in here."

He bent on one knee beside his bag and rummaged through it. "Light."

I angled the flashlight above him. He pulled out some bolt cutters and snapped off the padlock. He opened the box as I sank to my knees beside him, the flashlight aimed limply at the insides.

It was like Connor's friends had shoved his whole life inside it. Letters, ticket stubs, an old harmonica, photos… everything. I went to pick up an old prom picture, but Logan stopped me.

"Touching potentially haunted objects? Not a good idea. You run the risk of possession."

I blinked, eyes wide. "*Possession*?"

Logan nodded. "Best bet—torch everything." He went for his bag again and pulled out a small bottle with a tiny stopper.

"White rose oil?" I shined the light in his face.

He winced in the beam as he cocked an eyebrow. "I'm impressed, Grey... Wait, don't tell me—you didn't just stop by the historical place. You hit the books as soon as I told you the road was really haunted, didn't you?" He snickered. "I wouldn't have pegged you for the nerdy type —I thought that was more your sister..."

I rolled my eyes and smacked him with the flashlight. "You burn off curses with white rose oil...common sense. Now get it over with, would you?"

Logan poured the bottle of white rose oil over everything. He flicked his lighter, but before he could drop it in, I pointed my finger and shot a flame into the heart of what remained of Connor's life.

Logan flinched, as the fire roared. "OI!" He hopped up to his feet.

I snickered as I stood, smirking, and brushed the dirt off my pants. I watched the contents of the box smolder. They quickly burned down to ash. It wasn't a normal fire...white rose oil set aflame was a sacred burning. Not just the stuff inside, but the whole box disintegrated down to nothing.

"Was that it?" I snorted. "That was too easy...you made this thing seem dangerous." I flicked the flashlight back in Logan's face. "Now what?"

Logan held up his hand to shield his eyes as he scowled at me. "Now..." He snatched the flashlight from my hand. "Connor's ghost should be at rest. But we need to make sure—"

I crossed my arms over my chest. "How are we going to do that?"

Logan heaved his ruck onto his back and waved me to follow him. "First, we head back to the truck."

The two of us hiked up the ditch and back onto the road.

———

By the time we made it back to the truck, I was gripping my side and out of breath.

Logan tossed his bag in the truck bed. "Okay, so now—

"Logan..." My eyes scanned the woodline, then slid back to the street. I squinted into the darkness, down the road where we'd come.

Something flickered in the dark.

I glanced at him. His eyes narrowed.

Then the temperature dropped dramatically. Like the October night forgot it wasn't the dead of winter. My breath came out in a misty cloud in my face.

"He's coming..." Logan muttered.

My blood went cold at the sound.

Logan held up his crowbar like a bat and started forward.

"I thought we took care of it?" I whispered harshly as I moved to stand with him, my crowbar raised.

"Well, obviously something else is keeping him here," Logan snapped back. He checked his watch. "We're running out of time," he muttered. He shook his head. "This isn't going to be good..."

Dread churned in my stomach as my breath clouded in my face. I peeked at him sideways. "What do you mean?"

Logan gritted his teeth but didn't answer, his eyes shifting along the road in front of us. "A vengeful ghost is like a rabid animal—impossible to reason with, unless you push the right buttons. But first we have to get him to hold still long enough to get him talking…"

I rubbed a hand over my forehead, squinting down the road, searching for movement. "Wait. I could possibly trap him—I don't know if magic works on ghosts, but maybe?"

Logan shook his head again. "Doubtful…and he has to show himself in order for us to—" He looked at me as an idea struck him. "We'll bait him," Logan said quickly. "Just like I did to draw him away from Soccer Mom."

I smiled. "He jumps out at cars!"

Logan nodded curtly, eyeing the road. We had a plan. "Get in the truck."

The two of us loaded up into the cab.

"You okay?" Logan jutted his chin toward my arm.

I forced a smile and shrugged. "I barely notice the pain with all the running and screaming."

"When we finish this, we'll fix you up." Logan revved the truck to life, switched on his high beams, and peeled out onto the road, driving full speed into the darkness.

I hesitated. "Uhh…what do we do when he jumps out at us?"

"Improvise."

"Great…are your plans always this well thought out?"

Logan winced and shrugged.

I rolled my eyes.

"Well, why didn't the burning work?" I demanded.

He shook his head, his face lined with his frustration. "It should've. But like I said: he's tied to something else."

I gritted my teeth and scanned the side of the road as we barreled down Bell Hill. I tried to remember what Zan had said. "Ghosts are tied to either objects or emotions, right?"

Logan nodded. "Unfinished business." He grimaced as we reached the end of the road. "Hold on." He cranked the wheel violently, yet expertly, turning us back around.

My stomach lurched. I made a face as the truck righted itself. He stepped on the gas, and we shot down the road.

"Like what?" I looked sharply at him.

His face was stony and grim.

I frowned. "You aren't telling me something."

He rolled his eyes. His grip on the wheel tightened. "Listen, Grey—"

There was a flicker in front of the headlights. Connor materialized, standing in the middle of the road, his wolfman mask grinning wickedly in the light.

"Logan..."

Logan stepped on the gas. The truck roared.

"Logan!" I squeezed my eyes shut, shoulders hunched and braced for impact. Connor vanished before we hit him. I turned in my seat to see whether he'd reappear.

Logan pulled the truck over and came to a hard stop that made my neck snap forward.

I stared at him, eyes wide and a smirk in the corner of my mouth. "Did you just run over a ghost?"

"Stay in the truck." He shoved the truck into park. Then he jumped down.

But before he could slam the door, I slid out after him.

Logan scowled at me. "Get back in the truck!"

"You're stuck with me. Get over it." I gripped my crowbar and wandered out into the middle of the street. "Now what do we do? We can't beat him to death. Do we try to talk to him?"

He stood beside me, his crowbar ready, his eyes alert. "Like I said, we improvise."

Connor appeared behind him.

"LOGAN!"

Before he could swing, Connor waved his hand and sent Logan flying across the road. Then Connor came at me, his wolfman mask curled in a nasty, bloody smile, its eyes glassy and dead.

I swung.

He disappeared and reappeared.

He blasted me yards away from him with such force I lost hold of the crowbar.

I scrambled to my feet. The truck and Logan were so far. The crowbar was lost in the darkness. I was alone.

Connor appeared.

For the first time, I could truly see him: The bruises on his toned, bare arms. The road rash burned through his ripped Guns N' Roses T-shirt. The black blood oozing from his stomach, his guts dangling limply from a gaping hole in his side. I hesitated, horrified by the state of him.

He rushed at me.

His hand grabbed my throat.

THNKS FR TH MMRS

It felt like ice crushing my neck, burning cold on my skin. I gaped at the air like a fish. Tears springing to my eyes, my hands tore at his arm. He was too strong. The mask stared at me, unblinking, with that manic smile. I didn't want to look at it.

Out of the corner of my eye, I saw Logan running toward us down the middle of the road. Connor lashed out his free hand, sending him flying back again. I tried to heat my magic in my hand, but I couldn't focus.

I needed to breathe. Desperately, my fingers grabbed at his wolf head. My vision blurred. I gasped for air. My brain needed oxygen. I was going to black out. I grabbed the fur of the mask and yanked it as hard as I could. He didn't even flinch.

Then something small and hard sailed through the air. It knocked into the mask and bounced off it. Connor's body exploded in a burst of cold smoke. I stumbled back, gasping and coughing. My hand still clutched the fur of the mask. I looked down at it. It wasn't a part of his specter.

It was real.

Logan ran up to me, panting and out of breath. His hand squeezed my shoulder as I doubled over, gulping up air. "You all right?"

I inhaled deeply, closing my eyes briefly, my free hand massaging my throat. I nodded and straightened. "What was that?"

Logan leaned on his crowbar and grinned. "Iron horseshoe. I keep a couple in the truck bed just in case. I couldn't chuck a crowbar at him from that far. Didn't want to risk hitting you, too." Logan scrunched up his nose. "Those things hurt."

I scoffed in amused disbelief. I licked my lips and inhaled deeply again. I held up the wolf head like an Amazon warrior. The smell of it was rank, musty and stale like rotting earth. "It's real. When you hit him, it kind of knocked him out of it."

Logan stared down at me, his brow furrowed. Then his face broke into a broad grin. "From the night he died… no one bothered to recover it." He took the mask from me to examine it. Logan shook his head. "The whole time I thought he was just keeping up appearances. I didn't think he was actually *wearing* the thing." He clapped me on the back. "Nice work, Grey. This is it."

I smiled weakly.

There was a roar in the distance. The both of us flinched. The roar of an engine.

We ran down the road, back toward the truck. The

headlights flashed on. Slowly, the truck turned and backed up, shining the high beams in our faces.

"Is that—"

"It's Connor."

"*What?*"

"RUN!"

The truck lurched forward, full speed. We scrambled off the road and into the ditch. The truck screeched to a stop beside us, revving the engine. We charged into the woods, Logan bellowing about how the jerk better not crash his truck into a tree, and me holding my side as another cramp bit into my ribs.

We crouched low in the branches, peering back at the road. The truck was still revving threateningly.

Logan shook his head. "Ghosts, man."

"What do we do now?" I panted, trying to catch my breath. My throat burned.

Logan snorted. "We burn the mask." He nodded toward me. "And that means, unless you've got a bottle of white rose oil on you..." His gaze shifted back in the direction of the road. "We need to get to the truck."

I gaped at him. That was impossible. I shook my head, trying to straighten my thoughts. "How are we going to get to the truck when he's driving it?"

"He's possessing it," Logan snapped. "He's not *driving* it."

I made a face. "And the difference is?"

Logan sighed a low rumble in his chest. "Okay, paranormal creatures—by definition are not natural, right? Most of the time, if they possess someone, or something,"

Logan started to trek through the woods, parallel to the road. "Then they are forced to follow our rules, you know? The rules of science."

I crinkled my nose as I struggled to keep up with his stride. "*What*?"

Logan groaned. "Think IT. I mean, I know you probably can't read, but you must've seen the movie, right?" he quipped drily.

Ignoring the insult, I frowned at the idea. "But—" I bumped into Logan as he stopped short.

A dark shadow stood in front of us.

Connor.

Logan, one hand on his crowbar, swung fast, slicing completely through Connor, who exploded in a puff of cold mist. The crowbar thunked against a tree. Logan choked up on the crowbar and adjusted the mask underneath his arm. "Apparently, he left the truck."

"We can't keep holding him off like this, can we?" I scanned the trees.

"No." Logan hurried to the road. "It won't take him long to regenerate. We gotta burn this. Now."

I ran after him, slapping away the branches as we plowed through the trees and hiked up the embankment.

He halted in the road. I came up beside him.

Connor appeared in front of us.

I recoiled at the sight of his face illuminated in the waning moon. He didn't look like a monster. He didn't look evil. He looked kind of like Cole: dark hair, thoughtful eyes...but one side of his face was ripped, shredded from the road.

Then he changed.

His sad eyes darkened. Rage marred his features, and he punched his hand through Logan's gut.

Logan yelled out in pain. He tried to swing the crowbar, but Connor grabbed his arm, pinning it back.

"Burn it." Logan dropped the mask at my feet with a low groan. He bent forward, clutching at his stomach, still impaled by Connor's fist.

I blinked stupidly, shocked by the gore.

Burn it.

I snatched up the mask.

Right.

I hugged the mask to my chest and ran for the truck, my feet pounding on the road, keeping pace with my heart.

I skidded to a stop as the air in front of me seemed to shimmer. Then Connor appeared, flickering in and out like bad TV static. Instinctively, I held out my hand; magic orange flame burned like an aura around my fingers. I flexed my hand, sending a burst of magic out at him. But it passed right through him. He didn't even fade, much less explode. And he lunged. But Logan was ready. He charged past me and sliced Connor with the crowbar. Instantly, he burst into a cloud of cold.

This was our chance. I moved for the tailgate, but I stopped, hand raised, suspended just above the handle.

I blinked.

And I wasn't me anymore.

There were three of them. Dark figures laughing in the darkness. At first I thought they were all boys, but the third one slipped back her hood as she tugged on a wolf mask, and I could see her white face and bright eyes snickering in the moonlight. Kelly. She'd come. But, of course, she had. This was her favorite game to play.

I approached them anxiously, and I spoke in a voice not my own. "Hey, are you sure we should be doing this? I mean, Frankie *crashed* last night. I don't think—"

Kelly, her laugh hidden beneath the wolf mask, skipped toward me, taking my hands in hers. They were warm and soft as she squeezed the cold from mine. "Aww, Connor...Frank's fine." She giggled, her mischievous snicker muffled by the mask as it leered at me. "You should've heard him in math class. Going on and on about the Bell Hill wolfman! You're a legend, and it's barely been a week!" She tugged me down the embankment and into the ditch, in front of the stream that led to the Tracks. The boys laughed and jumped down after us.

My stomach clenched uncomfortably. "My point exactly...we can stop now."

The two boys flanked on either side of me nudged and shoved me with good natured teasing. I wasn't listening. Kelly rolled her head, the wolf mask leering at me in the darkness of the woods, and she pulled my mask from behind the culvert. I opened my mouth to argue, but she yanked it down over my head. Then she straightened my jacket and slapped my arm. "You look good, boyfriend."

My breath came hot and stuffy in my face as I squinted through the mask. It had started out as a joke. It's what island kids did...with nothing to do, no supervision, and underdeveloped prefrontal cortexes, we thought up crazy things to pass the time...or to impress and entertain each other. And Kelly...I'd do anything for her.

But last night everything had gone wrong. It had been Kelly's turn. She jumped out into the road at the oncoming car, but she'd ran too far out and instead of simply swerving into the other lane or slamming on the breaks, Frankie had had to crank it too far, too hard, to keep from hitting her. His Jeep flipped. I thought he was dead. I ran out of the woods from our hiding spot, tore across the street, the boys charging after me. The three of us flew past Kelly who stood frozen in the middle of the road, her wolfhead sneering, and together, the boys and I pulled Frankie out of the Jeep. He was all right. Just shaken up and freaking out. He tried to point to the road, but Kelly had vanished.

We'd walked Frankie home so he could call Eddie Martin for a tow. And he was okay. But I hadn't slept that night. And now, here I was...doing it again. For what? The joke stopped being funny the moment Frankie had flipped.

The boys huddled in the shadows of the woodline. Kelly slipped her hand in mine and pulled me toward the grassy slope of the embankment to wait. She dropped down to the grass and pulled me down beside her. "You and me, Connor. We're Nile legends."

It was Kelly.

I was doing it for Kelly. Because after her dad had run

off with his second family up in Quebec, I'd promised her I'd always be there. I'd never leave her. Not like him.

"Yeah..."

She tilted her head, her wolf mask slipping askew. "What's wrong, Conner?"

I didn't answer. I didn't want to disappoint her. This whole wolfman thing was some kind of romantic high for her. And I really wanted to make her happy.

Her sigh was muffled in her mask. She looked down at the grass, the mask sliding low, the wolf snout touching the grass. "Look, I know what happened to Frank messed you up...after tonight we'll stop, okay?"

"Really?" I scoffed. "You don't, like, think I'm a wuss or something?"

She turned her head, the wolfhead grinning wickedly at me. "Never. You're my guy, Connor McCallum. Whatever you want. Where you go, I go."

I snorted. "So, you won't leave me for Robby St. Claire?"

Kelly giggled. "Nope. You don't have to worry. I'll never leave you."

I grinned. "Back at cha, babe." There was a flash of headlights as a car turned onto the road. I straightened my mask and got ready to run.

13

MISERY BUSINESS

The car didn't swerve.

The front bumper slammed into me.

I flopped onto the window, rolled off the side, and smacked into the asphalt. It hurt so much that it didn't hurt. And I knew that was bad. The car didn't stop. It must've kept driving. Because it was dark all around except for the sky. The sky was brilliant, a black blanket of white pinpricked holes. And it was cold. So cold. And alone. My breath puffed like exhaust above my face. Why was I alone? I blinked furiously, as I stared wide eyed at the sky. Black velvet, every star, a puncture. Alone.

Then the memory shifted. And I wasn't Connor anymore. I was looking down on him, and I wondered if this was what it was like to die. Then Kelly dropped down beside him, her mask forgotten on the road, and I could feel the warmth of her love as Connor's loneliness melted away like slush on the street. She cradled Connor's head into her lap, smoothing back the sticky hair from his bloody face. Then she mumbled inaudible words of comfort through the stream of tears leaking from her blurring eyes.

And then I was back on Bell Hill Road, standing beside the truck, my hand frozen in place above the tailgate. I lowered my hand and turned to Logan.

"Grey..." Logan held out his hand. "give me the mask."

A white hot burn of rage surged through me like a wildfire. I wanted to kill him. I pulled my wand from my hair and slipped the mask over my head.

I pointed the wand at Logan. He backed up, his hands held high.

He was speaking, but I couldn't hear him.

I never could hear them.

I slashed the wand through the air, sending a stream of fire at him. But Logan was ready. He jumped to the left and scrambled around the side of the truck. I straightened the wolf mask and started after him. I didn't need to run. I would catch him. The chase was half the fun. He didn't go for the truck. Instead, he booked it down the grass slope and into the woods.

I grinned.

I loved it when they ran.

I flicked the wand over and over, shooting flames into the underbrush. I moved through the trees and stopped just inside the woodline, my eyes shifting from side to side. The mask made it almost impossible to see, and I squinted through the mesh, my breath puffing hot in my face.

Then there was a roar from the road. The truck. I let out a low, rumbling growl and turned around, headed for the street. Logan revved the engine, exhaust pouring out and surrounding the truck like dense clouds. His eyes met mine as I hurried up the embankment. Then he stepped on the gas and sped away down the road, tires screaming on the asphalt and red tail lights blinking in the dark. I stepped slowly out onto the street, my eyes on the shrinking glow of the truck. I didn't stop until I reached the middle, planting my feet on the yellow lines. I watched as the truck whipped around and sped my way, the engine roaring and tires screeching.

I smiled as the truck barreled toward me. Maybe he wouldn't stop? That would be interesting. I dropped the wand to the ground as I felt the fury fester and foam in my gut, bubbling to the surface and blinding my eyes. I hated them and their cars...always thinking they could scare me.

Not on this road.

I inclined my head, the wolf mask tilting slightly as Logan slammed on the breaks. The truck screeched as it jerked to a stop just beside me. Then Logan kicked open the door with a loud creak. He jumped out with something in his hand, low like a dagger. It was shadowed in the headlights, yet somehow I knew it was dangerous. The blind anger and hatred consumed me, and I attacked. Fingers curved like claws, I lunged at him. I scratched and tore and shredded.

Logan struggled against me. I was too strong. Inhumanely strong. Insane. Possessed. I laughed, high and cold, in a voice not my own. He wouldn't hurt me. Not while I was her. But then I felt a jab in my arm, and I collapsed. I was laying on the road, staring up at the stars. Just like that night. When it hurt so much it didn't. When I was all alone, on the cold, hard road. Alone with the stars. And I screamed out in agony.

Then the anger left me like a whoosh of a deep exhale, and I gasped as Logan yanked the mask off of my head and tossed it to the side of the road. He jabbed me again. I hissed through clenched teeth as I eyed the needle warily.

"What was that?" I moaned, my voice sharp with irritation.

"Mandrake."

"Mandrake." I repeated stupidly. My eyes widened as I glared up at him. "Do you know what that does to witches?"

"Yup." Logan snickered. "I told you. When ghosts possess something, all rules apply. It was the best way to get you on your butt." Logan paused as he considered something with a thoughtful frown. "I don't know what made him leave, though...I was expecting a battle for your soul," Logan quipped with a smirk. "Don't worry. I would've saved you." Logan chucked the shot off to the side, and he bent down, hooked his arms underneath my armpits, and scooped me up, shoving me onto my feet.

I staggered a minute.

"Congratulations." Logan clapped me on the shoulder sending me stumbling over my own feet. "You just survived your first ghost possession." Then he marched over to the mask and picked it up, panting slightly. "All right. We gotta torch this thing. The oil. It's in the trunk."

I put my hands on my forehead and tried to focus. I was me. Not Connor. And I needed my wand. I shuffled a bit in the shadow of the headlights and finally found it with my foot. I bent down to scoop it up and the blood rushed to my head. I groaned as I straightened.

Logan nudged me. "You good?"

I winced. "No."

Logan laughed and gave me another shove. "Come on, Grey. We burn this, and it's all over. Let's go."

Logan went around the truck. But before I could follow, the air beside me shimmered like a wavy channel change. I stuck the wand in my hair and hurried after Logan. He yanked open the tailgate and ripped through his bag.

I glanced over the side of the truck. "Hurry."

Logan pulled out a bottle of white rose oil.

"Quick!" I hissed, my voice hoarse.

But, he wasn't quick enough.

Connor appeared behind him and punched through Logan's back. Logan grunted, his teeth grinding on his silent scream and blood leaking from the corner of his mouth.

I winced at the strangled sound. Logan thrust the bottle into my hand as he dropped the head at my feet once more. I didn't dare touch the mask. My shaky fingers fumbled with the bottle stopper. Got it. I dumped the oil over the mask. Heart pounding in my ears, I pointed my finger, and shot fire at the wolfhead.

It burst into white flame with a loud roar.

I looked up.

My heart dropped into my stomach.

It didn't work.

Connor shoved Logan aside with such force he tossed him to the side of the road. He watched me through the burning white fire separating us. He bared his teeth, rotten and foaming, into a gruesome grin. Then he flickered like a fuzzy picture on an old TV. My breath clouded in front of my face.

The fire died down.

And Connor McCallum stepped toward me.

14

LIGHT UP THE SKY

It wasn't the mask.

The mask wasn't holding him here. And I had no idea what to do next. I stared at him, at what he'd become: eyes black and murderous, skin decayed. And my heart ached with empathy for the boy he'd been.

"Connor..." I held out my hands in surrender. "I'm here to help you. You've got to—"

His face curled into a nasty sneer. He launched himself at me, but I was ready. I whipped my wand out of my hair and sliced at him. He disappeared and reappeared at my side. He slashed at me, I dodged. Then in one quick motion, I stabbed the wand through his heart. It was like punching through a cold fog as Connor collapsed in on himself.

Panting, lungs and calves burning, I bent and helped Logan to his feet. "Are you okay?"

Logan scoffed, his hand holding his stomach. He wiped the blood from his chin. "No."

I tried to laugh, but it came out strained. I put a hand to my forehead. "We did it..." I laughed again, sounding a bit delirious as I rambled on, "We did it! But he still won't leave! Why won't he leave? The mask didn't work!" I blurted the obvious.

"Yeah, I see that." Logan screwed up his face as he forced himself to straighten. "We gotta figure out what's keeping him here."

I nodded quickly, licking my lips. I tried to focus, my thoughts still jumbled from adrenaline.

Logan reached into his rucksack and tossed me a water bottle. "Drink. It'll help your nerves."

Scowling, I twisted off the cap, swiping strains of sweaty hair out of my eyes with the back of my hand. "I'm fine," I snapped before I guzzled half the bottle.

"Let's go, Grey." Logan nudged my shoulder, and I sloshed water down my front.

Glaring at him as he headed around the truck to the driver's seat, I cranked the cap back on the bottle and chucked it in the back of the truck.

"Wait." I blurted the word before I could stop myself.

Logan stopped and turned to cock an eyebrow at me.

"I think we need to head into the woods."

Logan titled his chin and studied me with narrowed eyes. "Why?"

I took a deep breath. "I think we should head back to the spot where he was hit...the spot where they were hiding that night. I just have a feeling..."

Logan frowned and closed the distance between us so he could tower over me. "You're going to have to give me more than a hunch...did you see something when he possessed you?"

I hesitated.

"Grey..." Logan scoffed with a sympathetic smirk. "You can't trust what they remember."

"What do you mean?" I asked uneasily.

Logan shook his head, massaging his temples as he thought. "All right. You take point, Grey. But, be warned. This is going to get messy."

"What do you mean?" I glanced up at him as we walked down the middle of Bell Hill Road, back toward the Tracks.

"There's nothing else left to tie him to this road," Logan answered grimly. "Which leaves—"

"Unfinished business," I muttered darkly. I shook my head. "With who?"

"Probably his girlfriend." Logan mumbled underneath his breath, "And it's not like we can get her here."

I shook my head as my thoughts clashed. "Wait. I still don't understand."

Logan was silent as we came up to the culvert. "It's better if you don't."

"What?" I snapped.

"Suffice it to say...we've still got a long night ahead of us." Logan continued to mutter something about therapy for ghosts.

But I didn't bother to ask him to explain. My breath caught in my throat, and I grabbed Logan's arm, yanking him into me. This was where Connor'd been that night. I tugged Logan to the side of the road, and I dropped down into the ditch. He jumped down after me.

He stood off to the side, his arms crossed as he watched me turn in a circle by the stream. "You want to tell me what you're looking for?"

My eyes scanned the blue-black darkness as I spun slowly. "As soon as you tell me what his unfinished business is…" I stopped to stare at the culvert. I walked toward it slowly, almost hesitantly. I reached around the side and felt through the tangle of bush branches. My hand rested on something soft and grimey.

I pulled it out and held it up for him to see.

Kelly's mask.

Logan's arms fell to his sides and he made his way over to me. He took the mask in his hands. He glanced over at me, his eyebrow raised.

I nodded toward the mask. "It's Kelly's. They were both scaring cars that night."

"Is that what he showed you?" Logan scoffed and looked back down at the mask with a shake of his head. "Okay, so we need to get him talking…and it's going to be hard."

"Why?"

"Because he's gone dark. Vengeful. Like I said before, ghosts like that are nothing but raw rage. Feral, like animals. You felt it." Logan nodded at me. "He probably can't even hear us, yet. And he won't, not until we snap him back to reality. Then we can talk to him. But when we get him talking…it's going to bring him to a whole new level of evil if we don't do this right. We need to convince him to leave on his own—you know, head into the light as they say...but it won't work if he's lying to himself about what he's hanging on to..."

I waved off Logan's explanation, only half-listening. "How do we get him to talk to us?"

Logan shrugged, but before he could offer an answer, Connor appeared in the middle of the stream. His whole state of being had changed. Before he had been completely corporeal, solid and real. Now he looked like a faulty projected image. Glitching. Static.

"Connor..." Logan started slowly.

Connor didn't even look at him.

Then I remembered...he couldn't hear us.

Instinctively, I snatched Kelly's mask from Logan's hands and jammed it over my head. Dirt, and I didn't want to know what else, tumbled down my face and hair as I squinted through the mesh mask. I held my breath as I stepped toward him.

Connor's face softened instantly. He shimmered once, and then his appearance solidified. And he looked like he had in life. His dark eyes confused as he watched me cross the stones to get to him.

"Connor..." I said softly, my voice muffled by the mask. "Can you hear me?"

He nodded slowly.

I exhaled in relief. "Good." I took another breath. "I'm here to help you, Connor."

Connor inclined his head in question.

I took another step closer, stopping just at the river.

"You don't belong here all alone on this road. This isn't where you're meant to be."

"You need to let go, Connor," Logan called from where he stood. "Let go and move on."

Connor swallowed and licked his lips as he considered this.

"Ask me anything," Logan offered, moving closer, cautiously, as though he were approaching a wounded animal.

I followed his example, the two of us closing in on Connor from either side.

Connor blinked rapidly. His eyes began to leak. He didn't look at us. I don't know whether he even saw us, or even remembered we were there. The air around him…it felt like walking into a freezer. He was radiating cold sorrow. Chunks of ice churned in the bubbling stream at his feet.

He took a shaky breath, still staring unseeing, straight ahead. "Where is Kelly?" Connor licked his lips and sniffed. He nodded his head. "I need to see Kelly before I can leave…"

"Connor…" Logan hesitated. He cocked his head to the side. "You know what happened to Kelly."

Connor turned his head slowly to stare at him. His head—it moved unnaturally, like a doll's head turning to the side on a perfectly straight neck.

"*You're a liar,*" he hissed in a voice that echoed and vibrated low. His thick dark hair waved like it was caught in an intangible breeze. His eyes narrowed.

He was going to hurt him.

"Connor!" I shouted, muffled in the mask.

His head snapped toward me, his eyes wide and crazed.

I swallowed thickly, my heart beating, panicked in my chest. I had to keep him calm. Keep him sane. "I'm so sorry, Connor...I'm sorry that this happened to you. You didn't want to jump out that night...you made a mistake and it wasn't fair."

Connor's lip curled into a nasty sneer.

I tried again. "I know you're feeling like you need to see Kelly. You need to see her because you don't want her to think that you left her alone...but she knows, Connor. She knows you didn't want to leave her. So, you can let go. You can move on."

Connor laughed, but there was no amusement in it. It was only cold. Hollow. "Move on? To what?"

"Nobody knows for sure," Logan said calmly. "But it's gotta be better than being stuck on a cold, lonely road forever, right?"

Connor's hands ripped at his hair. He scratched at his face, and he screamed in a rage, "Stop. *Just stop talking!*" Connor's eyes flashed. He tossed his hand out toward Logan, his fingers curled like a claw.

Logan sank down to the bank of the stream, his knees wet in the water, his hands at his throat.

"Connor!" I cried out, my voice thin and weak in the face of his fury. "Stop! Look at me! Look at me, Connor!"

His eyes slid slowly from Logan to me.

I tugged off the mask so he could see my face. I inhaled sharply, my mind racing. My blood pounded loudly in my ears. I held up my hands in surrender. "Connor...you're hurting Logan. You need to let him go. I know the kind of person you are and this is not it. You have to remember how it felt when you were on the side of the road...when you were scared and didn't want to hurt anyone! You are not a monster. You need to stop—now. *Please*."

Connor lifted his hand, releasing Logan.

Logan doubled over, his hands splashed into the water as he braced himself, bent over on all fours, gasping and coughing.

I licked my lips. I could do this. "What are you holding on to, Connor? What's keeping you here?"

Connor blinked slowly, as if he were confused by the question.

Logan groaned as he struggled to his feet. "Don't bother asking him, Phoenix." He wiped his hands on his jeans. "He's not going to admit to anything."

Connor's eyes burned black as they slid toward Logan.

"Logan..." I eyed him warily. "You're not helping."

Logan shrugged. His kind, patient demeanor was gone. He was back to his usual snarky and big-headed self. "He's not either."

I sputtered, unable to think of a retort. What was he doing?

"He says he can't remember—but the truth is he doesn't *want* to remember...do you, Connor?"

Connor's black eyes narrowed. He vanished and reappeared, buzzing like static. The lights of the truck flickered. A cold wind rushed at us from all sides.

"You know what happened to Kelly."

"No," Connor hissed through rotting teeth.

Logan didn't stop. "She came back here on the anniversary of your death to leave flowers and a marker by the culvert. And you killed her."

BOIS LIE

"**N**O!" Connor's scream blasted against us like a shock wave coursing through the air.

Logan didn't flinch. "Catherine Kelly Barrow drove down this road on October 11th, 1986, a year after you died, and she was never seen again—" He stared Connor down, disgust etched in the lines of his face. "Because you ripped her to pieces—"

"I SAID NO!" Connor flew at him, his hands flexed like talons. He attacked him, scratching and cutting viciously with unnatural speed and strength.

I grabbed my wand from my hair, wishing I still had the crowbar, and sliced it through the air, aiming at Connor. "*Incaendium!*"

The magic passed right through him. I ran at him then, wand out like a knife.

I slashed at him.

Connor exploded in a cloud of mist, covering me in icy-cold smoke.

I coughed and waved a hand around my face to clear it. I stabbed my wand back into my hair and reached for Logan just as he collapsed, his knees buckling underneath his weight. I bent beside him, my eyes moving over him, assessing his injuries. Blood, black in the moonlight, gushed from gashes in Logan's shirt and jeans. He looked pale, deathly pale. He struggled to stay conscious; his eyelids fluttered, droopy as he swayed where he sat.

I shook my head. "What the hex were you thinking? *Are you seriously as dumb as you look?*"

Logan tried to scoff, but he could only manage a weak exhale. He struggled to swallow and licked his lips. "He's in denial...no matter what we did...I had to push him—so we could figure out what's keeping him here."

My heart hammered in my head, as I struggled to think of how to help Logan.

He groaned through gritted teeth. Then he forced a smirk and looked at me with heavy eyelids. His words came out in a labored pant as he asked, "Any—any...chance you can...uh, wiggle your nose...and—uh, heal me up, Grey?"

I winced. His wounds continued to leak black blood. "N-No. My mom—my sister...I—I don't know how to—"

Logan scoffed again with a pained smile. "Figures I'd get the Grey with no talent."

My eyes prickled hot. "Logan—"

"Help me up," Logan said gently.

I nodded quickly, happy to have something I could do. I stuck my hands underneath his armpits and yanked him to his feet.

"I've got...bandages...in the truck," Logan panted.

"Great..." I mumbled as I grunted underneath the weight of him and together we climbed up the ditch and onto the road. The truck wasn't too far. Logan had left the lights on and we limped toward it as fast as we could considering the state of him.

Finally we made it to the bumper and I helped him stumble to the tailgate. My eyes darted around the dark shadows, waiting for Connor to reappear. "Where do you think he is?"

Logan shook his head as he leaned gingerly against the truck. I pulled down the tailgate and dug through his bag, emerging with an old, beat-up first-aid box.

"Like I said, he's in denial...faced with a truth like that..." Logan paused to take a breath. "It'll take him a minute to gather himself again." Logan shifted his weight on the truck.

"Why didn't you tell me about Kelly?" I unlatched the box and rifled through the contents.

"I was hoping to avoid it...kind of unsettles the stomach, don't you think? Ghost Boyfriend Rips Girlfriend Apart in a Blind Ghosty Rage...not a headline I want to read more about..."

I passed him some bandages, and together we patched him up as best we could.

"Grammy—my uh, grandmother...I can take you to her. She should be able to—er—put you back together again." I recoiled at the sight of his wounds, raw and dark in the harsh taillights.

Logan winced and shook his head. "Nah, I know a guy."

"So, what is Connor's unfinished business?" I shrugged, struggling not to feel defeated. "And how do we use it against him?"

Logan leaned against the truck again, trying to catch his breath. "It could be anything...it's not looking good for us."

"So—let's go over what we know. He killed Kelly...but he was a ghost then...he was already hanging around... maybe it has to do with the car that hit him...or something Kelly said to him while he was dying—"

"No—" Logan groaned through clenched teeth. "Hey, do you remember where those crowbars went?"

"Uhmm—" I checked the truck and glanced down the road. "I think we left them...somewhere."

Logan scoffed. "Great."

"What do you mean, 'no?'" I prompted.

Logan inhaled deeply, his nostrils flaring. "Grab a can of salt from the ruck—I should have at least one..."

I snatched at his rucksack, dug out a can, and put it in his hands.

He cleared his throat. "Uh, no—" Logan blinked, as though he were trying to focus. "No Kelly. I talked to the guys...Connor's buddies...they said Connor went there alone that night. No one was with him. Hit and run. He was found the next morning. He bled out on the road by himself." Logan shook his head with a grim scowl. "It took hours. The coroner's report said he was paralyzed by the impact but it took hours for him to lose consciousness."

I let out a little gasp at the horror of it. Then my brow furrowed, and I scrunched up my face in confusion. "That's not what he thinks happened…"

Logan poured out a handful of salt and held it out for me. "Fill your pockets. Salt repels them a bit…not as strong as iron, but…improvise, right?"

I took the salt, only half paying attention. I was missing something. "Why doesn't Connor remember what happened?"

"Heh. Some ghosts are in denial, only seeing what they want to see."

"Only what they want—because the truth is too painful?" The pace of my heart raced with my train of thought.

Logan nodded. "That's why I reminded him about Kelly—"

"Because the truth could kill him!" I gasped, hopping a bit from excitement.

Logan's brow furrowed as he smiled in pained, perplexed amusement at my enthusiasm. "Right—but it didn't…because like you said, he was already a ghost by the time he killed her, so it's something else." Logan held his side. "And we are screwed. Royally." He jutted his thumb behind him toward the front of the truck. "Grab me a water, would you?"

I ran around to the cab and hopped halfway inside to snag the bottle from the cup holder.

The radio started to crackle.

The cab lights flickered.

The autumn air plummeted into winter coldness; frost

crinkled the water bottle, gripped tight in my hand. My breath came out in a puff of hot mist as I slid slowly back down to the ground.

The radio fizzed.

Connor's voice hissed through the stereo, *"He's a liar!"*

I snatched my wand and spun around. Nothing was there. I took a deep breath. He wasn't there.

Then there was a grunt. And a thud.

The truck rolled slightly forward on its braked tires.

My heart dropped into my stomach.

Logan.

I ran around the truck.

Connor had his hand stuck inside Logan's gut, pinning him to the tailgate. Impaled on his arm, Logan was hunched over.

He wasn't moving.

I charged at Connor with my wand like a dagger.

I stabbed at his head.

Instantly, he burst apart, showering me with black, icy smoke. I grabbed Logan's arm and tugged him roughly back up to his feet. I slapped at his face.

His eyes fluttered open.

"Oh, thank God," I gasped. "You're alive."

He sagged in my arms. He couldn't stand. And he was heavy.

"You're going to sit," I snapped. Logan tried to argue. I ignored him. My hand on his shoulder, I shoved him down to the ground. His knees buckled, and he dropped on his butt.

Logan held his gut and looked up at me with a wince and a cocked eyebrow. "What was that—your knitting needle?"

I inclined my head.

He nodded toward my hand, his breathing shallow.

"Oh, my wand—it's forged from magic iron…"

Logan tried to laugh. "And here I thought witches didn't like iron, either."

I wasn't listening. My eyes darted around the lonely road. Connor would be back. I needed to keep him away from Logan. I needed to end him. And now I knew how.

"Left—" Logan grunted at my feet.

I turned quickly, slicing at Connor with my wand. He exploded in a cold shower of mist that made my teeth chatter.

Not a second later, Connor appeared a few feet from us, out of reach of my wand. I stabbed it in my hair and moved toward Logan, but his power froze me in place.

Connor's eyes pierced into him. His face contorted with his rage. His skin was patchy and decomposed, the white bone of his jaw bright in the waning moonlight above us. He reached his hand out low, aiming his power at Logan still on the ground.

"I know what happened Connor!" I shouted loudly. "I know the truth…"

Connor froze, his eyes moving up to meet mine.

I took a shaky breath, my heart aching for his pain. "Logan's not the one who's lying…is he?"

Connor's face darkened. The air around him crackled, and an icy wind began to blow.

"It was your friends. They lied...they were there that night..."

Connor lifted his hand.

I was pulled toward him. My Converse skidded on the street as I tried to hold my ground. It was impossible. He dragged me to him.

His hand closed on my throat like an icy vise. My skin burned cold and my eyes blurred with the pain. Connor lowered his face so he was just a breath away from me. He bared his black, rotten teeth, his eyes dead and glassy.

"And so was Kelly," I choked out, as he crushed my throat.

Connor screamed in my face, so loud it felt like my brain was melting.

I grabbed my wand from my hair and slashed. Connor vanished before I could hit him.

"BEHIND!" Logan bellowed from the darkness.

I whirled around to see Connor, his head bent low, eyes hard and teeth grinning in a manic smile that stretched too wide. He punched out his fist and clenched his fingers at the empty air.

I screamed and bent over my stomach. I could feel him. His power crunched my insides, ripping and tearing.

I had to keep going. "But it's worse than that—" My voice was thick with blood, as it gurgled and dripped from my mouth. I moaned in pain. Gritting my teeth, I met his gaze, my eyes burning bronze. "She broke her promise, didn't she?"

Connor flickered; his hold on me vanished.

I gasped in relief.

I spat the blood from my mouth. I hugged my gut, still keeping my eyes on his. *"Kelly left you...she ran away...all of them did...and you bled out on the road all alone with the stars."*

THAT'S WHAT YOU GET

"**N**O!"

Connor's scream slammed against me, sliding me back a foot.

I didn't flinch. "That's why you're haunting this road."

Connor flickered, his body shimmering in waves like static.

"That's what tied you to Bell Hill Road. Your heartbreak."

"NO!" Connor slashed his hand through the air.

Invisible nails sliced my arm. I grabbed my shoulder. Blood, hot and thick, oozed over my cold fingers. I didn't stop. "Did she check on you first? Did she think you were too far gone before she ran away to hide her mask?"

Connor roared, slashing his hand again and again.

The cuts tore into my arms. I gritted my teeth. But my eyes didn't leave his face. "She promised she'd never leave you..." I had to push harder. I had to hurt him. Like putting a wounded animal out of its misery. "But she did —and I'll bet she didn't even look back."

Connor looked up to the sky. He let out a tortured scream that ripped through the night. Then his body shattered in an explosion of blinding white light.

And he was gone.

My hand dropped from my shoulder, hanging limply at my side. I stared at the place where he'd been, the empty road illuminated in the light of the sinking moon. I blinked. I couldn't focus my thoughts. I could only stare stupidly at the road.

"Grey...you all right?"

I looked up.

Logan.

I winced as I started toward him, walking slowly, painfully back to the truck. I hurt inside and out. All over.

I spat. The metallic taste of blood still coated my tongue.

Logan limped along the length of the truck bed. "You did good, Grey." Logan nodded his approval. "Get in the truck."

I made my way to the passenger side, sliding in as gingerly as I could manage. Logan, on the other hand, wasn't as gentle with himself. He grabbed the wheel and yanked himself up into the seat with a rough grunt.

He moved just slow enough that it was clear he was in a lot of pain. Even if he didn't make a sound. His jaw tightened as he cranked the keys in the ignition. The truck roared to life, and Logan pulled away from the side onto the road.

"You're hurt—I know a guy. He'll check us out before I bring you home, okay?" Logan glanced at me sideways.

I shrugged weakly.

Logan gave me a kind smile. "Like I said, you did good. Especially for your first hunt."

"Yeah? I don't feel good," I mumbled, staring moodily out the window at the passing blur of black trees.

"Psh—I've seen worse...you'll live." Logan grinned.

I scowled. "That's not what I meant."

Logan made a face. "Then what?"

"Kelly left Connor—dying on the side of the road and all alone...because she was afraid of getting in trouble."

"Yeah, his buddies didn't waiver in their story, either—"

I scoffed, disgusted. "They left him there. He didn't even want to be there. He was doing it for her...and she just left him there."

Logan nodded, scowling. "Yeah, I hear you." He glanced at me with a sideways smirk. "Nice work putting that together, by the way. How'd you figure it out?"

I shrugged. "The memory was different. And you said he saw what he wanted. He made up the ending the way he wished it had happened." I winced at the image. I shook my head. "I can't believe she left him like that..."

Logan nodded grimly as he turned down another road.

I was quiet the rest of the way to the ferry. All I could think about was Seraphina. Whatever happened, whatever we said to each other...she'd never leave me like that. But then...she was already gone, wasn't she? I glared out at the ferry docks as Logan pulled up and parked to wait for the boat to come back across the lake.

He drove us to Mater Christi High School. Apparently, the guy he knew was the principal, Father LaValley. If not for his title and the fact that he came out the back door of a rectory, I would've thought him some kind of police officer or something. The man was muscular in a toned, fit way...his T-shirt tight on arms etched with tattoos swirling up and down the length of them. I studied the markings as he approached.

"Those are witch runes—" I looked up at him in surprise.

His kind, handsome face split into a smile. "Spellwork. Protective." He set a box down on the tailgate. He popped it open, revealing bottles and jars and numerous other obviously supernatural first-aid items.

He held out his hands toward my arm. "May I?"

I lifted my left arm for his inspection.

He moved his hand through the air, hovering over the wounds. "Vengeful spirit, eh?"

"You should see the other guy." I jutted my head toward Logan, who leaned against the truck beside me.

LaValley laughed.

Logan scoffed and winced. "Keep talking, Grey..."

I gave him a sly smirk, as LaValley started to apply a salve to my wounds.

"I need to ask—" LaValley caught my eye with a paternally stark stare. "Does your mother know what you've been up to tonight?"

I cocked an eyebrow.

LaValley chuckled. A pink tinge pinched his tan cheeks. "I had to ask...school principal and all... Speaking of..." LaValley glanced at Logan, as he finished applying the salve to my arms. "There's something going on, something I can't put my finger on...you on it, Logan?"

Logan nodded curtly. The motion made him wince.

LaValley put the bottle back into his box and rummaged through it. "Good. It's not like anything I've seen. Something's off." He handed Logan a belt. "Bite."

I raised a curious eyebrow as Logan bit down on the belt.

LaValley lifted up Logan's shredded shirt with one hand and held up a thick, giant needle with the other. "Three—" He stabbed the needle deep into Logan's stomach before he could say two.

Logan groaned, his jaw taut and trembling, as though he struggled not to scream. His breathing came fast and labored, wheezing through his clenched teeth.

LaValley gave a grim smile and patted him on the back of the head. "Good man. Like looking at your daddy."

Logan nodded stiffly, scowling through the pain. His breathing came in halting puffs.

"All right." LaValley took the belt from Logan's mouth and put it back in his box. "Hard part's over." He selected a bottle and started to smooth the salve on Logan's cuts. Logan's nostrils flared as he continued to pant.

"You look like a dragon," I said dryly.

Logan's eyes slid to mine with a murderous glare.

I laughed.

LaValley hid a smile. He cleared his throat and kept working on the wounds. "So, I assume you've had your eye on Seraphina..."

"It's not her," Logan muttered. "Pretty sure..."

My ears prickled, and I straightened off the truck. "What about her?"

LaValley nodded quickly. "Of course it's not. And I'm glad you're watching her. She could potentially be a target...considering—"

Logan and LaValley exchanged a pointed look.

Then Logan nodded again. "Heard."

"Wait—" I sputtered, increasingly annoyed that they were talking in code about my sister. "What are you guys—"

"All set, doc?" Logan asked, ignoring me.

LaValley grinned. "All set. Now get out of here before Sister Francis spies the both of you and starts asking questions. That woman—"

"Wait a minute!" I snapped angrily.

LaValley gripped my shoulders and looked deep into my eyes. "You take care of yourself, Phoenix Grey. It was a pleasure to finally meet you."

Then he released me and gave Logan a nod of approval. "Your old man would be proud."

Then he grabbed his box, snapped it shut, and headed back to the rectory without another word or backward glance, leaving me gaping and blinking stupidly in his wake.

"Get in the truck, Grey." Logan pushed off the truck, grabbed my backpack, and slapped up the tailgate.

He heaved my backpack easily as he shoved it into my arms. I winced underneath its weight and slung it over my shoulder as I studied him. He was no longer panting or struggling to move...I inclined my head. His wounds were gone. Though his shirt and jacket were still stained and tattered, his skin was smooth underneath the dried blood caked all over him like rust. I looked down at my arms, gingerly poking my fingers in the holes of my hoodie and the tears in my tank top. Healed, without a blemish, let alone a scar.

Logan hopped in the driver's seat, and I hurried to the passenger side, slightly dazed at the miracle. I dropped my bag onto the floorboard at my feet. Logan cranked the truck to life. Wasting no time, he peeled out of the driveway and sped onto the road. The sky was purple with the morning twilight as we headed toward the ferry.

I glanced at the clock. Seraphina would be waking up soon. What would she think when my bed was empty? Would she care?

"Hey—" Logan snapped me from my moody thoughts. "It's over, okay? You gotta let it go."

I rolled my eyes and glared out the window.

"Seriously, you can't carry baggage in this business. It'll weigh you down and get you killed..." Logan scowled. Then he cleared his throat and jabbed his finger into the CD button. Asia blasted from the radio.

I flashed him a sugary, sweet smile. "Ahh, great song—"

Logan glanced sideways at me with a small smirk. "Yeah?"

"Yeah—if you're *sixty*." I snickered at his scowl. "Now, what were you guys saying about my sister?"

Logan's jaw tightened. He ignored me, continuing to glare at the road ahead.

"I'll keep asking...it's a long drive to the ferry. Long boat ride..."

"Get your phone." Logan nodded to my pockets. "I'll give you my number in case you run into trouble again."

"I don't have a phone."

Logan stared at me in surprise.

My cheeks burned. "Cell phones can interfere with magic," I muttered defensively. "And besides, if I was in trouble, you'd be the last person I'd call."

"Seriously?" Logan smirked. "You and your sister don't have phones?"

"We don't have a TV, either," I snapped. "And because of that, our brains will survive the mass mind-melting and overall decay of society. So, we win."

Logan scoffed.

I smacked his shoulder as he stopped at a red light. "What were you saying about my sister?"

Logan rubbed the back of his neck. "There's something evil going on in Nile... So I've been keeping an eye on your sister."

I scrunched up my face. "Yeah, you said that...so you're watching her—to like, what? Keep her safe?"

Logan snorted. "Something like that..."

I frowned, my eyes narrowed. "You're making sure she doesn't go dark...aren't you?"

Logan's jaw tightened, but he didn't answer. The light turned green, and he kept driving.

"That's it," I said accusingly. "You think she'll go wicked. Unbelievable." I shook my head, folding my arms across my chest. I kicked my feet up against the glovebox and muttered to myself.

"Oi!" Logan slapped at my sneakers, knocking my feet from the glovebox back down to the floorboard.

"I should hex your ears to your butt," I blurted coolly.

"*What*?" Logan scoffed, screwing up his face, as though he couldn't believe what I'd just said. "Listen...the thing about witches—they don't always have the strongest moral compass, okay? And I'm sure she's a sweet girl...you know, with the hair and the smile, and all that, but it's easy for a mistake to turn—"

I gritted my teeth, my fingers clenched into fists at my sides. "Just stop. Stop talking. *Now*."

"See?" Logan nodded toward me with a smirk. "You want to jinx me right now, don't you?" He shook his head, as he reached underneath the seat for a crumpled-up paper bag. "Believe me..." He shoved his hand into the bag and fished out a cookie. "I've hunted plenty of witches and—" He took a big bite and mumbled around the crumbles, "Sure, okay, they may start out like Samantha Stephens, all hot and housewifey, but in the end—*Endora*." Logan gave a sarcastic shiver.

I pursed my lips together in a disgusted pout. "You're

just seeing what you want to see, DeVarney. You talk a good game, but really...you're just a bigot."

"And you're just a hag." Logan held up a cookie to me in mock salute. He flashed a sweet smile.

"*Auribus—*"

Logan stuffed the cookie in my mouth before I could finish my hex. "Eat. Maybe the sugar will sweeten that sour disposition of yours."

I shot him a cool look as I snatched the entire bag of cookies from his lap. Logan laughed.

Seething, blood practically boiling, I stuffed my hand into the bag and munched one cookie after another. I hated that they were delicious.

Logan cranked up the radio. I winced as Kansas moaned in my ears. By the time we pulled up onto the ferry boat and parked, the sun was rising at our backs, casting a warm glow along the lake. My temper had cooled, but only slightly.

"Whatever," I mumbled through mouthfuls of cookie. "My sister may be a bit lost, and going through some kind of teenage life crisis, but she would *never* go wicked."

Logan shrugged, with a satisfied smirk on his face. "We'll see...I hear she threatened to hex a few kids at school already...hate to see what she gets up to at that sleepover this weekend."

Sleepover? My face twitched.

"Ahh—you didn't know about that, did you?" Logan chuckled darkly.

I frowned, seething in silence. I turned away from him and watched the gray waves slosh and spill over the boat deck. My stomach hurt, and it wasn't from all the cookies. A sick feeling of dread had washed over me, and now I was sinking in it.

And it was all Logan's fault.

I hated him for making me question her. And when he finally pulled up to Grey Cottage, I snatched my backpack, slammed the truck door as hard as I could, and ran up the porch steps without ever looking back. But I couldn't run from the feeling that maybe he was right.

Phin *had* changed. She was angrier. Distant. And maybe it had something to do with that school...maybe she *would* go wicked...turn her back on me, like Kelly did to Connor...summon a demon, make a deal for dark magic...

But whatever was going on with Phin, whatever happened, I knew one thing for sure: I never wanted to see Logan DeVarney again.

And if I ever did, I would finish that hex.

This story holds a special place in my heart as it was
written especially for you.
If you enjoyed *The First Hunt of Phoenix Grey*, let me
know when you leave a review.
And don't forget to post a picture!

Inspired by episode 2.16 of *Supernatural*, I wanted to take
the haunted road story and fit it into the Nile Universe.
But instead of a highway, it had to be a backroad.
Backroads are always spooky—the isolation and loneliness
of a two-lane dirt road are much more scary than your
average country song might suggest.
Also, the part about Connor scaring cars at night...totally
happened. But his name wasn't Connor—and thankfully
he didn't die...but he could've—so please, dear reader, tell
your friends: don't be dumb like Connor McCallum.
And while we're at it: don't be evil like Kelly, either.

This is the end of *The First Hunt of Phoenix Grey* but the Grey sisters' journey into the supernatural world has just begun!

So...

What is going on with Seraphina at Mater Christi High?

Will she really go wicked?

And what will happen when Nix sees Logan again?

Find out in *Seraphina Grey Summons a Demon.*

Coming Spring 2024

Hi, I'm Cristine!
I love old sitcoms and slasher films.
When I'm not writing, I'm playing Animal Crossing or
Harvest Moon 64.
When I am writing, I like to write dark fantasy with a light
heart. This means I want to disturb you without leaving
you feeling yucky at the end of the story. In short, I'm
inventing a new genre I like to call 'cozy dark fantasy.'
My books are heavily influenced by my experiences
growing up wild on an island in the middle of the lake.
Almost all the things I write about are inspired by real
life...but for legal purposes— that's a lie.
To read more lies and see photos of the things that *did not*
inspire my writing, sign up for my newsletter at
cristinecourcy.com/newsletter.

Connect with me online:

WWW.CRISTINECOURCY.COM

goodreads.com/cristinecourcy

facebook.com/cristinecourcy

instagram.com/cristinecourcy

threads.net/@cristinecourcy

youtube.com/@cristinecourcy

x.com/cristinecourcy

tiktok.com/@cristinecourcy

amazon.com/author/cristinecourcy